FACE TO FACE

"I'm going to show you how the Cheyenne settle with a man who's taken what's dear," sneered Ashley. "Devlin, I want you to know what it feels like to lose an arm—or two. Maybe a leg! I might just start with the fingers, shoot off each of 'em as it suits me. So what do we start with, Devlin? Fingers, toes, an ear maybe? Well, Devlin?" Ashley yelled, cocking his pistol.

"Ears first," he whispered, laughing. The others echoed their approval. Willie winced.

But before the pistol could fire, a wild cry split the air. . . .

Delamer Westerns by G. Clifton Wisler
Published by Fawcett Gold Medal Books:

STARR'S SHOWDOWN

THE TRIDENT BRAND

PURGATORY

ABREGO CANYON

THE WAYWARD TRAIL

SOUTH PASS AMBUSH

Sweetwater Flats

G. CLIFTON WISLER

FAWCETT GOLD MEDAL • NEW YORK

A Fawcett Gold Medal Book
Published by Ballantine Books

Library of Congress Catalog Card Number: 88-91298

ISBN 0-449-13360-5

Manufactured in the United States of America

First Edition: January 1989

for Ann Jensen
teacher, colleague, friend

CHAPTER 1

Spring in the Rockies was a season of renewal, a time for rebuilding, of clearing away the old so that new life might spring forth. A winter chill still haunted the air, and snow stubbornly clung to rocky crevices and nestled around the bases of cottonwood and spruce trees. Even so, the first wildflowers began to splash patches of blue and yellow across hillsides. Ground squirrels scampered about. The newborn deer appeared shyly in the thickets while their mothers kept a wary eye out for hunters.

Willie Delamer welcomed the changes. Winter had been bitter cruel. Once again it had brought death and darkness. Its shadows had left him cold, had painted his world with ice and pain.

Now it's spring, those shadows will pass, he told himself. Already, as the sun smiled down on the glimmering waters of Rock Creek, he thought he tasted something bright and promising. There was a scent of hope on the wind.

I've deemed it so before, he thought. There's only been disappointment . . . and death. But as he drank in the marvels all around him, he wondered. There beside him, scooping the sandy bottom of the creek in a shiny flat pan, stood Vance Bonner. Only seventeen, and barely five and a half feet tall stretched head to toe, Vance took to the hunt for gold flakes with a rare devotion born of youthful enthusiasm. With the straps of oversized overalls draped over his bony shoulders and his trouser legs rolled up above the knees, the boy seemed oddly frail.

Size didn't make a man, though, Willie told himself. Vance had all the heart and grit required. Willie only hoped nature and fate would provide the time needed to grow broad shoulders and a whiskered chin.

Old Gump Barlow had enough whiskers for the whole valley. The years Gump had panned streams and dug out hillsides were nigh past numbering. He knew every inch of the Sweetwater country, from South Pass to the Medicine Bow. The old-timer's silver hair and wrinkled brow attested to the trials of a mountain life. But spring had painted a smile on old Gump's face as well, and Gump sifted the creek bottom and swapped jests with Vance.

Willie did likewise, though he had no particular fondness for gold or silver. They usually brought trouble. Wealth couldn't buy either happiness or peace, and they were the only commodities of any true value. He panned the stream anyway. Something within him cried for company, and despite the frigid sting of the icy creek, Willie felt warm sharing the labors of friends.

A short way downstream Mathilde Bonner hung up the weekly wash on a rope stretched between two cottonwoods. Even from a distance her amber hair warmed Willie. He knew she was likely grumbling about the work and cursing men in general, but that fierce independence of hers only endeared Tildy Bonner to him all the more.

Most days she'd be down at the creek, too, panning with the best of them. Tildy didn't care too much for scrubbing clothes, but neither could she tolerate the seedy appearance her companions quickly acquired when washing was left unattended.

"You want my clothes clean, wash 'em, Sis," Vance had remarked.

"Seems fair to me," old Gump declared.

"And what about you yourselves?" Tildy countered.

"Am I to take my brush to your hide as well?"

The men had promptly agreed to a weekly bath in consideration of Tildy's services as laundress. Other chores, such as cooking and cleaning, were parceled out in turns, though. Willie usually dodged them by taking to the hills in search of meat for the meal table. Sometimes Vance would grab a rifle and follow along. More often Willie went alone. Solitude provided a balm of sorts for his growing apprehension. Willie felt Tildy carving a place for herself in his heart. Vance more and more was becoming the younger brother left behind a decade before in Texas. And Gump seemed the father whose sage counsel had been silenced forever that awful April evening near the Tennessee River, when honor and valor had been revealed for the hollow words they were.

Willie swept all that from his mind as he moved the pan in a slow circular motion so that by and by the sand separated itself from pebbles and the occasional yellow sparkle of a gold flake. Ten years ago placer mines had emptied Rock Creek of her true wealth. Now spring runoff from melting snow sprinkled a bit of gold here and there. The big mines at South Pass City and Atlantic City—the nest of tunnels known as Miner's Delight—were mostly abandoned. A few scavengers dug through the leavings, extracting an ounce or two now and then. Most had given up.

Since departing the stage station and freight depot operated by Tildy's grandfather, Willie and his little company had drifted up Willow Creek, passed the ghost of Atlantic City, and settled in on Rock Creek. The small cabin that gave shelter from the cold was made of planks borrowed from collapsed stores and houses. In time it, too, would be left behind.

Downstream two families, the Moffats and Hagens, shared a camp formed by canvas hovels. A pair of ancient wagons turned on their sides provided a windbreak. Willie sometimes brought them rabbits or an elk roast when the hunting was particularly good. At such times he would look past the glittering eyes of the men into the sad, hollow faces of the women. There Willie read the agony and despair of life in a gold camp. Ragged, barefooted children labored to shovel sand into sluice boxes. Occasionally the wind would carry sorrowful voices whining somber tunes of forlorn hopes.

Willie had seen it all before. The mountains whispered peace, but more often they provided a great chance for failure and death. He vividly recalled the morning the Murphy gang had ridden down on the camps at Willow Creek, just beyond South Pass City, sowing death like a Kansas farmer tossed seed. There were the Sioux, too. Tom Reed, the young lieutenant who led cavalry patrols out of Ft. Stambaugh, related how the twelve-year-old son of the post commander had gone to fetch the family cow. When the boy hadn't returned, soldiers sent to find him had stumbled across the boy's frail body, his young heart pierced by a dozen arrows.

"Life here is bitter hard," Gump was fond of saying. "But there's a freshness to the air and a sweetness to the earth. She gives us the gold and silver buried in her heart."

Gump would speak of the heyday of South Pass City, when millions were dug from the hills, and fortunes were made. Those tales were mere echoes of a voice long dead now.

"We'll make our fortune, too," Vance assured Willie. "Wealth and riches'll be ours."

"I've known life in a gold camp," Willie answered. "There's little of either for very long. Mostly it's hard work digging out the gold, and harder labor afterward trying to keep it from those who'd take it away."

The tedious hours spent panning the creek did nothing to change Willie's mind. A month's labor filled only one small rawhide pouch.

"There's time yet," Gump declared.

Willie wondered.

As he sat on the hillside watching the sun fade into the distant mountains, he wondered what gypsy wind had blown him so far from his native Texas. In his dreams even now he heard the thundering hooves of buffalo he'd hunted as a boy of fourteen. He recalled the surging waters of the Brazos in spring flood, and he walked the ancient burial grounds atop the Castle Cliffs, recalling friends laid to rest, dreams set aside.

Little remained of the boy who'd run bare-shouldered across a hard, parched land, dreaming of great herds of longhorns and the yellow-haired girl who would walk always at his side.

"I don't even have my name anymore," Willie muttered. Now he was Wil Devlin, just another wayfarer doomed to wander abandoned claims in search of that most elusive of all treasures. Not gold. Peace.

It was hard to come by along Rock Creek.

A little before midday the riders came. Willie counted three. Then a fourth emerged from the pines on the hillside. They moved slowly, cautiously, up Rock Creek before stopping fifty yards short of the cabin. Tildy stepped over to where a loaded Winchester rested beside a skinning rack. Willie left Gump and Vance in the stream and joined her.

"Howdy there!" the lead horseman called.

Willie eyed them all with suspicion. Their bearded faces betrayed no hunger. Each of the strangers was wrapped in a heavy buffalo-hide cloak. A small cannon could lurk beneath such garb. The thought offered Willie no comfort. They brought along no pack mules, no supplies of any kind.

"Name's Tracer," the leader added, examining the camp. His gaze fell on the rifle Tildy passed to Willie. The stranger's eyes avoided Willie thereafter.

"Devlin," Willie answered at last. "This is my camp here."

"Pannin' the creek, eh?" Tracer asked. "I was down this way not so long ago. Year or two back. They were pullin' nuggets the size o' your fist from these hills."

"I don't recall seein' you," Gump grumbled. "I was here then."

"Fine prospects back then," Tracer continued. "Lot o' men made their fortunes along the Sweetwater. We been thinkin' there might be some color left in these old creeks."

"Found much yourselves?" a second rider asked.

Vance started to answer, but a frown from Willie silenced the young man.

"Hardly worth troubling ourselves over," Willie commented. "Truth is, we've been talking of moving on."

"That's right," Tildy agreed. "We're out of near everythin' you can think of. I've hardly got enough sugar to last out the week, and we can't even offer you a cup o'coffee."

Willie nursed the rifle with one hand, then motioned Vance out of the stream with the other. The boy paused a moment, but Gump gave him an encouraging nudge toward the bank.

"Things that bad, how come you to stay this long?" Tracer asked, staring at Gump. "You got the nose for color, don't you, old-timer? What's that you got in that pouch tied to your belt?"

"Let's see it," the second rider added.

"You wouldn't care to mess with a man's personals," Willie argued. "That's a Shoshoni medicine pouch. Only thing better looking hanging from a man's belt'd be a pair of scalps. Or," Willie added, staring icily at the intruders, "four."

"You keep a Shoshoni woman, did you, Grandpa?" Tracer asked. "I hear them Shoshonis know where every yellow rock in tarnation is hid. Care to share the secret with your friends?"

"My friends know everything I do," Gump replied. "You wouldn't want to number yourself among 'em, fellow. I'm a bit pickier who I keep company with."

"Are you?" Tracer asked. "Look at yourself, old man. You've got a snip of a girl and that boy there. This fellow with the sour face might make a fighter, but the others—

well, they're little use. Team up with us, and we'll all be rich."

"I been rich," Gump grumbled. "Didn't like it much."

"Maybe you just didn't know how to go about it," Tracer suggested with a grin. "We'd show you how, wouldn't we, boys?"

The others nodded enthusiastically. Gump slowly shook his head and splashed his way out of the creek. Willie tightened his grip on the Winchester. The rider on the far left moved around behind Gump, and the one on the right turned toward the cabin. Tracer and the other man stepped down from their horses. Their smiles faded.

"We mean to do some business this day," Tracer insisted. "You folks can make it easy or hard."

"Nothing's ever been easy," Willie answered, stepping back so that he stood between the riders and Tildy. At the same time Vance eased his way toward Willie's saddle. A spare pistol rested in a knapsack underneath. The boy was still several feet away when the left-hand rider whipped out a pistol and fired. The shot went wide, but Vance nevertheless threw himself to the ground.

"Now that was just plain stupid!" Tracer howled at Vance.

"Sure was," Willie barked, turning his rifle and firing in reply. The shot sliced the reins from the left-hand rider's hands. The stranger's horse bucked him into the creek and raced off. The other rider tried to draw a pistol, but Willie waved the rifle in that direction, and the horseman galloped away.

"Hold up, friend!" Tracer pleaded. "We mean you no harm."

"Mister, I'm particular about the people who call me friend!" Willie shouted. "You're lucky not to be short half your company already. Now, you open up those buffalo cloaks and drop your firearms. Understand?"

"The devil we will!" Tracer shouted.

Willie fired, and the Winchester sent a projectile just past Tracer's left ear.

"You got exactly one minute," Willie told them. "I don't see those coats off and the guns tossed free, I take some serious steps. Well?"

Tracer's companions obediently discarded their coats and tossed aside their weapons. Tracer did likewise. Vance eased over and collected the arms.

"You can't leave a man to ride Sioux country unarmed!" Tracer objected.

"I could leave you dead instead," Willie reminded them. "Most would. Now, I look around in another minute and find you're still here, I'm apt to leave you just that way. Some buzzard's sure to eat well tonight if I do. Hear?"

"I hear just fine," Tracer said. His smile vanished as he stepped carefully to where his horse had strayed. His companion helped the thrown rider along. The three men then scrambled atop their horses and prepared to ride off.

"You're makin' a mistake," Tracer called. "We'd made you a fair proposition."

"That right?" Willie asked. "Well, I'll make you one. Get clear of my sight before I put this Winchester to its proper purpose."

"Let's go!" Tracer said, trotting to his horse. But as the three retired, Tracer turned and yelled a final challenge to Wil Devlin.

"He's right, Wil," Gump complained. "You did make a big mistake."

"Gump?" Vance asked.

"I seen it all before," Gump declared. "Gold brings out the worst in some men. You may be real sorry you didn't shoot the bunch of 'em."

"Couldn't," Willie explained. "I don't think this rifle has but one more shell in the magazine. Besides, I couldn't be sure somebody else wouldn't get caught up in the fight."

Vance frowned. Tildy grinned and rested a hand on Willie's shoulder.

"They may come back," Vance whispered.

"Could be," Willie admitted. "Me, I hope not. Winter's brought enough killing to these mountains. Spring's best put to other work than digging graves."

CHAPTER 2

Thereafter, Willie never left the cabin without a pistol strapped to his hip and the Winchester loaded and waiting nearby. If he went hunting, Gump would stand watch over the camp. Even the most harmless-looking visitor to Rock Creek found himself greeted with suspicious eyes. More often than not, those eyes glanced down the sight of a loaded rifle.

The Moffats and Hagens kept a like vigil at their camp downstream. Willie detected traces of fear amid the despair in the eyes of the children. Soon there was hunger as well.

"Isn't just these hills that're played out," Gump remarked. "Game's gone, too. Soldiers shoot anything that moves along Beaver Creek. Their scouts hunt down all the elk west of the fort, and only a man not fond of his hair sets off north or east. Sioux don't show much sign o' turnin' friendly, Wil."

"So what're you thinking?" Willie asked.

"Maybe it's time to head on," the old-timer confessed.

"No," Tildy argued. "Gump Barlow, you said there still might be a fortune to be dug out of these hills!"

"That was before," Gump grumbled. "Now we're here, I see every inch o' this country's been mined. This old earth just has nothin' left to give."

Even so, Willie and the others continued to sift the

creek bottom. Fewer and fewer flakes remained when the pan was emptied of sand. The days grew longer, with little or nothing to show for the effort.

"I wish we'd never left Grandpa's place!" Vance stormed after a long day's panning netted less than a thimbleful of gold. "This creek's cursed, if you ask me! Look at us. We're all half-frozen from wadin' this icy water. My hands and arms and legs are wrinkled like some old frog-faced squaw! I've likely stunted my growth. And what do I have for company? Ol' Gump and his tall tales! Tildy's bossin'! And Wil Devlin's prowlin' 'round at night, givin' everyone to think some grizzly's apt to storm inside the cabin any minute!"

Vance sent his pan skimming downstream and splashed his way to the bank. The boy continued muttering and cursing for half an hour. Willie laughed, retrieved the errant pan, and waved Vance over.

"Does a man good to blow off some steam now and then," Willie said. "And I wouldn't worry about grizzlies. Human critters are a whole lot more likely to trouble us."

"That sure helps me sleep better, Wil," Vance replied, frowning and shaking his head. "You're a true comfort, you are."

"I try to be," Willie said, grinning.

He knew it was only the impatience that came with being seventeen that set Vance to raving sometimes. A few days profitable panning would revive young spirits. A bit of sunshine would bring out the color in Tildy's cheeks and ease Gump's miseries. But April remained chill and somber. Gray mornings flowed into hazy afternoons and gloomy evenings.

We'd be swimming the river back in Texas, Willie thought as he fought to shake off the bite of the icy stream. But Texas was a world away, lost in a universe of regret and disappointment.

Tildy recognized the pain that flooded Willie's face whenever the wind whined through the cottonwoods.

"I sometimes remember things, too," she told him. "I

see Ma and Pa in the shadows, remember friends, even my baby sister. Just ghosts is all, nothin' to bother yourself over."

"Nothing?" Willie asked, blinking away faces of fallen friends, nightmare scenes of death and destruction. "I've known a world of pain, and it's never far away."

She gripped his hand tightly and led the way outside. The wind ate at their faces and drove icy daggers through their ribs. Willie drew her against him, and they sat in the shelter of an abandoned stamp mill.

"Ever thought of building a good life, Wil Devlin?" she whispered.

"A good life?" Willie asked.

"One that goes somewhere. With someone."

"I came here, didn't I? With you, Gump, and Vance."

"With us, Wil? Are you really with us? Everytime I look over and see you, you seem farther and farther away."

"It's probably best," Willie said, turning away. "You don't know me. I wouldn't make you happy."

"I want to know you."

"Can you be so sure? You call me Wil Devlin. That's not even my name! Remember when I first rode into your grandpa's station? You thought me likely to be the worst kind of renegade. You were closer to the truth than you thought."

"Once maybe. Not now," she said, resting her head on his shoulder.

He closed his eyes a moment and tried to erase the ghosts haunting his thoughts. There were too many to vanquish that quickly, though. He shuddered off an image of long ago, reopened his eyes and stared overhead at the twinkling stars.

"So?" she asked. "Tell me."

"What?"

"Everything," she said, intertwining her fingers with his. "Who are you? What have you done? Everything."

Willie took a deep breath, then coughed. It was a long tale, and he didn't wish to share it. There was an urgency to Tildy's touch, though, and he suddenly surrendered.

"My father gave me his name," Willie began. "It was his father's as well. William Delamer."

"So the Wil part's true enough."

"Yes," Willie admitted. "About all that is. I was born in Texas, back in forty-six, the first of my family to come into the world after Texas became part of the United States. And for a time, it seemed no one else would."

"You grew up there?"

"I was raised along the Brazos River. I rode horses, worked cattle, hunted, and fished. My father had great plans for me. He thought I'd one day run our ranch. But I guess it wasn't to be. I never was much for civilized ways, and when he decided to send me to school in New Orleans, I ran off to live with the Comanches."

"Comanches! Wil, I never knew them to take in white boys."

"I owed that to Papa. He fought Yellow Shirt for years. Then the two made a peace. I grew up hunting with the old chief's son, Red Wolf. I think our fathers hoped we'd keep the treaty they'd made in their hearts."

"Did you?"

"No," Willie said, shivering as he recalled carrying the body of his old friend to the burial cliffs. "I came back to Papa. Then came the war, and nothing was ever quite the same afterward."

Willie paused only long enough to catch his breath. Then he spoke of battle and blood, terror and death, the long four years that seemed to choke all the good from his world.

"Others fought in the war, Willie," Tildy scolded. "You survived."

"Did I?" he asked. "For me the war's never really come to an end. The enemies change. The battlefields move. But it's the same story really. Blood and death. And afterward there's a chill which grips my heart!"

"So you drift."

"As fast and as far as I can."

"It's a poor way to live, Willie. Aren't you tired of running across the range like some range pony, scampering away every time anybody comes close?"

"Is that me?"

"Isn't it?"

"I suppose so," he admitted. "And maybe it always will be."

"I don't believe that, Wil. Once you thought to return. I remember your story of the yellow-haired girl. And so do you," she added, taking the small locket from his pocket and opening it. Even now Ellen's solemn face and blazing eyes made him tremble.

"She's married, with a house full of kids. And I'm . . ."

"What?"

"Alone."

"Not anymore," Tildy objected. "Not ever again, Wil."

"You don't know what you're bargaining for. I've grown old, and there's little tenderness left to give a woman."

"I've known my share of hard times, too, Wil. I'm not so young myself. You've been like a brother to Vance since you arrived at Grandpa's."

"I close to got him killed twice."

"Saved us all, you mean. You did it again when those four men rode up the other day. Wil, I've roped wild mustangs before. And ridden 'em, too. You won't shake me."

"It would be better for you if I could," Wil warned.

But she didn't hear those words, or perhaps refused to pay them any mind. They sat together as the wind continued to whine through the nearby cottonwoods. Wil thought it a mournful, haunting tune. Tildy only smiled and gazed at the moon anchored over the mountains.

In the days that followed, Willie felt her eyes on him often. His mornings began with her smile and ended with a somber nod as they took to their blankets.

"We'd best hunt up a preacher 'fore summer hits," Vance said, laughing at the two of them. "Be good to marry 'fore you're old and gray, don't you think?"

Willie tried to ignore the young man's goading. He confessed his strong feelings for Tildy Bonner, but the old doubts didn't fade. Each rider splashing across Rock Creek threatened to disrupt the springtime tranquility. And the long days of increasingly fruitless panning warned soon it would be time to move on again.

From dawn to dusk Willie and Vance worked the far bank of Rock Creek while Gump and Tildy sifted the sandy near bank. Willie's fingers began to grow numb, and his feet nearly froze when the shrill wind and gray clouds swept away the April sun. Up and down the creek they worked, wearily plucking golden flakes from the mud and sand. A day's efforts managed a spoonful of color on a good day.

Downstream the Moffats and Hagens fared even worse. With children to feed and clothe, their needs were greater. The Hagen's thirteen-year-old, Seth, confided to Vance how hunger gripped his brothers and sisters.

"If not for the trout we catch in the creek, we'd starve sure," Seth later told Willie. "There's never enough dust to pay our bill at Haybro's. I haven't tasted a biscuit in weeks now."

But when Willie spoke to Seth's father of leaving, Ethan Hagen sadly shook his head.

"One place is as good as another for seekin' gold," Hagen countered. "We place our faith in the Lord. He'll lead us to prosperity."

Willie shook his head. Faith was a powerful tool. It got a man through the worst that life could send his way. But it never fed a hungry child or fended off the icy, heartless fingers of death.

Some nights, sitting beside the fire and chewing a bit of venison or perhaps one of Tildy's biscuits, Willie could close his eyes and listen to the sorrowful notes echoing from downstream. Althea Hagen and Janie Moffat would blend their high, sweet notes and speak of the trials of struggling. Old trail songs always spoke of some final destination. No one in a gold camp could look forward to trail's end. There was only more struggling . . . or death.

Gump Barlow would bolster their spirits by telling of old times spent trapping the Green River. As he spoke of Jim Bridger, of tracking grizzlies or eluding Sioux and Cheyenne raiders, Vance would close his eyes and grin. Willie knew the youngster was dreaming of adventure in a way now lost to his elders.

Strange how alike they are, Willie thought as he watched Gump and Vance. An old man's memories merged with a young man's dreams. Both were, in a way, a distortion of reality. But what other amusement was to be found along Rock Creek?

Now and then Willie took a turn at tale spinning, too. His stories were usually of Texas, of better days spent on horseback or chasing Ellen Cobb through the shallows of the Brazos. And there were also the stories of his days in the Comanche camps.

"Now all that's left of Red Wolf and his people are the shadows chasing buffalo ghosts across cattle ranges," Willie muttered. "Their ways are dead, stolen by strangers, erased by anger and misunderstanding."

"So it is with the Shoshonis," Gump added. "When I first came through South Pass, they rode fierce and proud, score upon score of 'em. Their camps were alive with the howls and songs of little ones. Buffalo and elk hides stretched on skinnin' racks, and horses by the hundred grazed near circles of lodges.

"I felt at home there. Once I was known as a hunter, a fair shot with a rifle who wasn't afraid, who killed for his own table and respected others; they welcomed me like an old friend. Better they should've fought. First the smallpox and then measles ravaged the tribe. Then came the Sioux. Now old men sing of past glory, and the young ones scout for the army or die drinkin' white man's whiskey. The camps are silent, 'cept for the sobbin' o' mothers for their dead children."

Willie nodded. He saw every bit of it, though he hadn't visited a Shoshoni camp since '66. And as he listened to the mournful voices of the Hagens and Moffats, he felt their pain.

"I'm going after fresh meat today," Willie announced that next morning.

"We've still got a shoulder of venison put by," Tildy reminded him. "You know we need you workin' the stream."

"Wasn't just thinking of our needs," he explained, glancing downstream. "Fresh meat would be welcome down there, I'd guess."

"I've got some flour, too," she offered. "Even a bit of sugar and coffee."

"They'll never take it," Willie insisted. "They're starving, but they haven't lost pride. It's one thing to take part of a neighbor's kill. To take supplies—well, I wouldn't judge they'd do it."

Tildy nodded sadly, then filled a small provision bag and waved him into the hills.

Willie rode half a mile before sighting a hint of game. The torn bark on cottonwood trees and discarded antlers half buried by lingering snow hinted deer were nearby. Willie found tracks near a small pond and set off in pursuit.

He located a small buck wandering a hillside a quarter mile from the pond. The animal seemed lost, and Willie judged it must have been sent on its way by a more dominant buck.

We're alike, we two, Willie thought as he steadied the Winchester and took dead aim. The deer seemed to spot the movement, but it didn't run. Instead a strange calm seemed to fall upon the animal. It held its head high, as if to sniff the wind. Willie fired, and the buck turned his way, gazed defiantly, then collapsed.

"Your pain's over," Willie whispered when he reached the fallen beast. "Your death will bring a shine to hungry eyes. Life will come of this."

As he cut away the skin and butchered the buck, he imagined the shining faces of the Moffats and Hagens. He envied the deer its swift and silent end. No good would come of his own, Willie guessed. Life would simply continue elsewhere, in the same whirl of pain and sorrow that choked the good and spread grief like a plague across the Rockies.

That image filled Willie's mind when he brought the meat to the canvas hovel a little before noon. Erma Hagen took the meat silently. Her husband, John and Clarice Moffat, and the older children merely nodded. They didn't pause in their toil to offer thanks, and Willie didn't solicit any.

Later that afternoon Seth brought a piece of wood carved in the shape of a horse.

"Not much payment for the meat, but some," the boy said, taking Willie's hand with his own. "Pa always says a man should pay his own way."

"It's a good way to be," Willie declared.

"Hard on the little ones, though," Seth added. "Little Peter's been sickly. I hoped Mr. Barlow might have a look. He's old, I admit, but he knows Indian healin' herbs and such."

"I'm sure he'd be glad to walk back with you, son," Willie said, pointing to where Gump stood emptying a few grains of gold into a pouch.

"Thanks again for the meat, Mr. Devlin," Seth said as he set off toward Gump. "Isn't just anybody'd find time to help when there's so much needs doin'."

Willie grinned, then kicked off his boots, removed his stockings, rolled up his trousers and waded into the creek. Tildy motioned for Vance to swap spots with her, and the boy splashed over to where Seth spoke with old Gump.

"More trouble in the Hagen camp?" Tildy asked when she reached Willie.

"Peter, the youngest, is ailing."

"You've taken those children to heart, haven't you?"

"Me? I worry about myself," Willie mumbled.

"Oh, you'd like everybody to believe that, wouldn't

you? Truth is you're as good as a Dutch uncle to those kids. You'd make a good father."

"No," he grumbled as he dipped his pan into the sandy bottom. "Fathers ought to stay around long enough to know their kids' names. Me, I'm a wanderer."

"Were. Not anymore."

"Always," Willie insisted.

"You sure?" she asked. "Forgotten our talk already? Wil, you can't drift forever. Think about my offer. It's a fair one. I'd make a good wife. I'd give you children and a permanent home."

"How long? What would happen when trouble came?"

"We'll face it together. *If* it comes."

"It will," he assured her. "What kind of a fool would bring children into a world of death and dying? The moment I find a place where I think I can be at peace, some ghost from the past always comes along to destroy it. I've cared about others, Tildy. I've buried most of 'em. I don't want that for you! I couldn't survive losing another family."

"Another one?"

"I held my papa's hand the night he died at Shiloh, Tildy. Mama—well, she passed on while I was away fighting. I've got a sister somewhere in Colorado, two brothers in Texas, but they're all lost to me, now."

"And Ellen?"

"She more than anyone," he said, shuddering as a rare chill tore through him. "I care for you, Tildy. Too much to let you make such a bad bargain. You don't know what you'd be getting."

"Don't I?" she asked. "You're not a stranger to me anymore, Wil Devlin or Delamer or whatever you choose to be called. Say all you want, but deep inside you know you want something different, something better. We could build it together. Don't turn away. Please don't!"

"It's a hard trail you'd take to, Tildy Bonner."

"I've known hard trails before," she replied. "You'll find me up to it. I'm not a piece of Philadelphia crystal you can break, you know. I've lived my whole life out here, weathered storm and flood, fought Sioux raiders and South Pass bandits. I've got enough grit for whatever comes."

"I know," Willie confessed. "You've got just enough backbone to get yourself killed. That's what worries me."

"You can worry yourself to death, Wil. Grab my hand, and let's build a future. I'm tired of bein' lonely. I want to start a family, carve out a place for a cabin I can know for home."

"Even if it's no better than what Erma Hagen and Clarice Moffat have?"

"They don't rest their shoulder against the cold come nightfall," Tildy said, tossing aside her pan and gripping his hands. "I long to hear my children sing come evenin', to feel whole, to belong to somebody. I want a real home."

"I'm not sure you'll find any of that with me."

"I am, Wil. You give me a chance, and I'll surprise you."

He sighed. Tildy Bonner was forever surprising him. And deep inside he welcomed the dream she painted of the future. It was a better place than any he'd known since boyhood.

"I'll try," Willie promised. "But in the end, it'll likely come to nothing."

CHAPTER 3

The work grew no easier. The fruits of that labor continued to be disappointing. The April moon was waning, and summer's approach revived Willie's spirits. New flowers invaded the hillsides, and the sweet songs of larks and cardinals serenaded Rock Creek's little community.

May brought other changes. The creek lost its frigid touch. Most afternoons Willie and Vance worked the stream barebacked. Sweat replaced chilblains.

"Soon there'll come an end to the runoff from the mountains," Gump pointed out. "Then we dig. Or quit."

"I'm for quittin'," Vance said. "We hardly get enough to pay for supplies now. This place's been dug and redug for ten years. There's no rich vein waitin' to be found. At best, we'll grind a bit of dust now and then."

"He's right," Willie agreed. "Come summer, we're apt to be swamped with newcomers as well, more families like the Hagens and Moffats . . . or scavengers."

"Here, we have the cabin," Tildy reminded them. "As for supplies, we're bein' frugal. Wil shoots fresh meat, and Vance is gettin' downright clever at hookin' trout. We do need some flour and coffee. Right now, as a matter of fact. But we can do without if it comes to that."

"Without coffee?" Gump cried. "I'm not a man to demand many pleasures, but I do care for my coffee."

"It's time someone made the trip to Haybro's then." Tildy declared. "I don't care to have gold sittin' around anyway. Wil, can you and Vance go?"

"You'll need him to work the creek," Willie answered. "I'll do it myself. What do you need?"

"I'll make a list," she said, grinning. "You'll leave tomorrow?"

"First light," Willie promised.

He did just that. The sun had scarcely cracked the eastern horizon when Willie climbed atop his horse and set off toward South Pass City and the little trading post Jonas Haybro operated there. Prices at Haybro's store were high, but there was little competition. Also, Haybro took unrefined gold in payment and would ship excess powder on freight wagons down to the railroad junction at Point of Rocks and eventually to the Merchant's Bank of Cheyenne.

Willie doubted there'd be much excess. He carried one of the three pouches Gump kept hidden beneath the cabin's floorboards. It never paid to let strangers, even Haybro himself, spy so much gold. It was little more than an invitation to trouble.

"There are men in these mountains who'd scalp their own ma for a pouch of gold flakes," Gump liked to say. "You watch yourself on the road, Wil. I thought I spied a pair of riders yesterday up on the hill."

"I'll be fine," Willie assured them before leaving. "I know these trails better'n most."

"But not all," Tildy scolded. "Keep your eyes out, Wil. Gump needs his coffee, and I need you."

Those words warmed him as he made his way downstream toward the narrow trail that traversed the hills lying between Rock Creek and South Pass City. A pair of shadows moved beside the creek, and sounds of splashing feet attracted Willie's attention. He eased his pistol out of its holster and nudged his horse toward the creek. There, wrestling in the shallows, were Ethan Hagen, John Moffat, and their five boys.

"Mornin', Mr. Devlin," Seth called as he slung a cake

of soap at his brother Alex. "You're up early."

"Headed for Haybro's," Willie explained, laughing as Jake and Clark Moffat applied a liberal amount of soap to their small brother Stuart's back.

"Buyin' flour?" Ethan Hagen asked. Willie nodded. "Might pick up ten pounds for me. I got some gold I can send with you."

"I'll get the flour," Willie said. "You pay when I get back with it."

"Fair enough," Hagen agreed.

"I can't help wondering why you're taking your bath so early," Willie added, shaking his head. "That water must be freezing so close to dawn."

"It is," Seth readily admitted. "I can't feel my toes, and Clark's backside is close to as red as his hair!"

"Is not," Clark protested. "Anyway, it may be warmer later on, but there are sure a lot less sisters spyin' on you now."

Jake nodded in an exaggerated fashion, and Willie laughed. Inside, though, he shuddered. Strange how simple things could remind him how far his path had strayed from his dreams.

"Well, I'll leave you to what peace you can find, friends," Willie finally said, leading his horse past them. Amid the noise and confusion that came with youngsters, Willie thought he detected a rare grin on Ethan Hagen's exhausted face. It was a marvel that joy could survive such hardships as spring on Rock Creek had brought those families.

Willie continued down the gorge, then crossed the creek and rode cautiously the narrow trail that threaded its way through the hills, past deserted mines and diggings, on toward South Pass City. He paused twice. The first time he spotted a fragment of cloth in the lower branches of a cottonwood. He thought it might mark some peril, but it proved to be just a bit of muslin, likely torn from the shirt of a Shoshoni scout or drifting miner. The fabric was cheap, thin . . . the kind often provided to Indian tribes as trade goods.

The second time Willie spotted tracks in the sandy soil. Horses, several of them, had recently come that way. They'd been ridden hard by the look of the tracks. Willie dismounted long enough to get a better look. Shod horses meant an army patrol, most likely. It seemed the soldiers were probably chasing Sioux through the hills again.

There were other possibilities, too. It hadn't been that long ago that Willie had tangled with the Murphy brothers only a few miles to the west. The Murphys were dead now, but other outlaws were known to haunt the Rockies. Gold drew them like buzzards.

As he continued, Willie tensed. Even the slightest sound merited attention. But as he traversed the trail across the hills and on toward winding Willow Creek, he found little to fear. Other tracks crossed his path—shod and unshod ponies, a cart of some kind, even a wagon—but he found no trace of any riders now. Suddenly there was a stirring in the brush to his left, though. Willie drew his pistol, then hugged his horse so as to present a smaller target.

For a minute Willie failed to detect the cause of his alarm. Then the lower branches of a small pine moved. Willie slapped his horse into a gallop and closed on the unknown peril. Only when five yards distant did he see an old mule bolt across the hillside.

"Anyone there?" Willie called as he searched out a rider. There was none. The mule bore no saddle, nor even a hint of a blanket. The animal was ragged, and its coat was tangled with every manner of burr and briar imaginable.

"Sorry to startle you, old fellow," Willie said, grinning as the beast bared its teeth. The mule had likely escaped the army or else had been abandoned years before by some miner down on his luck. Willie chuckled at the notion that a weathered old mule had almost sent him scurrying for safety.

"Well," he declared, "better to be overcautious than overdead."

Willie was still laughing when he began the sharp descent toward Willow Creek. He could see smoke from the breakfast fires of miners a few miles to the west now. A community of miners clung to Willow Creek and the South Pass diggings. Willie judged most would be gone before summer's close, though. The leavings were not worth wintering in the Rockies.

Twenty feet short of Willow Creek Willie again heard a sound. He quickly detected three shadows on the far slope. No escaped mule emerged from the trees this time. The shadows spread out along the ridge.

Willie knew they were men, but for a few moments he hoped they held no danger. He called out—in English and in the smattering of Shoshoni and Sioux he recalled from his year in the Bighorn country. No one answered.

He started to turn, but a single figure on horseback appeared on the trail. The stranger's grizzled face seemed somehow familiar. A great buffalo-hide cloak concealed the rest of him. There wasn't a hint of friendship in the rider's dark, menacing eyes.

"That's close enough!" Willie warned, drawing his pistol.

"Is it now?" the stranger asked, edging closer. "I'd guess that was for me to decide, Devlin."

"I know you?" Willie asked, examining the sour face for some clue to its identity.

"We've met before," the stranger continued. "You put a bullet in me."

"I've done that plenty," Willie said, swinging his pistol toward the oncoming rider. "I told you to stop!"

A rifle barked out from behind then. Willie steadied his horse and turned to spy three riders emerge from the cover of a nest of pines. A like number rode out from the far ridge.

"Drop it!" the rider in the trail demanded. "Now!"

Willie glanced anxiously around him. There were six

rifles trained on him now and no hope of escape. He cast the pistol aside.

"Remember now?" the bearded stranger cried. "Remember how you shot me? Where?"

"Kansas?" Willie asked.

"You cut a man in half and don't even remember it? Curse you for that, Devlin!"

"Was down south of here," Willie said, recognizing the bitter glare in the man's eyes.

"Point of Rocks."

"Your name's Asher," Willie declared.

"Ashley. Shadrack Ashley. I'll make more of an impression on you this time, I promise."

"You were drunk that day," Willie said, recalling the scene. Ashley had drawn a pistol on another, and Willie had put a bullet through the villain's wrist. "You drew on an unarmed man! You're pure lucky not to've killed somebody and got hung for it. As it was, I only clipped your arm. Another might have shot you dead."

"You should have!" Ashley shouted. "Before the sun sets, you'll wish to heaven you did!"

"You're a fool to carry a grudge," Willie argued. "You're lucky it was me shot you."

"Lucky?" Ashley screamed, flinging his cloak aside. Only then did Willie notice the empty right sleeve. Shad Ashley's arm was gone from the elbow down. "Lucky?" Ashley cried again. "I look lucky? I passed most o' my life ridin' guard for gold wagons. Later I hunted buffs. Buffs're gone, and Pop wasn't hirin' one-armed men. You've left me but one path, and you want me to thank you? Go to blazes."

"No, Shad," one of the others argued. "We won't leave him to do it on his own. We'll deliver him . . . in pieces."

Ashley grinned for the first time.

"You know my friends, don't you, Devlin?" the one-armed rider asked. "Seems they owe you somethin', too. You took some guns off 'em, I understand."

"They rode down on my camp," Willie said, swallowing the bitter taste in his mouth. He recognized the four would-be raiders. Gump had been right. Letting them go had proven to be a mistake.

"Guess now that pretty gal's back there all by herself," the raider on the far left declared. "When we finish here, Shad, why don't we go pay her a visit? There's just a snip of a boy and an old man left there."

"That old man's Gump Barlow," Willie growled.

"Barlow, eh?" Ashley asked. "And the boy and girl? Couldn't be they're Pop Bonner's grandkids? I owe the all of you. I settled up already with Pop himself. That station burned real nice. Now—well, why waste all this on a dead man? You let your imagination figure it all out. Old Gump and Pop's grandkids! We'll have some sport left for tomorrow, boys!"

The others cheered. Willie felt something die inside him. Then Ashley rode over and jabbed the barrel of a rifle into Willie's ribs.

"Down!" Ashley ordered.

Willie slid off his horse, and the animal scrambled off toward the creek.

"Fools!" Ashley screamed. "It's gotten away."

"We don't need horses," a burly man with a notched leather hat insisted. "Ain't anyone out there to warn."

Ashley slapped the man, then dismounted to face Willie. The others followed. Two men led the horses down to the creek for a drink, leaving Ashley and the four who'd visited Rock Creek to tend Wil Devlin.

The outlaws began by snatching the gold pouch from Willie's belt. They then removed the gun belt, flung aside a buckskin jacket, knocked his hat to the ground, and tore open his shirt.

"You seen trouble before, haven't you?" Ashley asked as he drove a fist into Willie's belly. "Not like you'll know today, though!"

Ashley slammed an elbow across Willie's forehead. A blinding pain sent Willie to his knees. One of the other outlaws kicked out. The toe of his boot struck Willie's spine, numbing his legs. The whole bunch then descended like wild dogs, punching and scratching, clawing... stripping off his boots and leaving him in a ball of fiery pain.

"You still feel anything, Devlin?" Ashley asked, kicking Willie hard in the ribs, then dragging him over against a boulder. "You see me?"

"I... see... nothing," Willie stammered through bleeding lips.

"I'm goin' to show you how the Cheyenne settle with a man who's taken what's dear. Devlin, I want you to know what it feels like to lose an arm—or two. Maybe a leg! I might just start with the fingers, shoot off each of 'em as it suits me. Then maybe your toes. You'll bleed slow that way. Then I can notch your ears, maybe cut an eye. I'll take pieces off you till there's not much left. Then who knows? Maybe I'll take you back to the Bonner girl so you can watch me do the same to her."

Willie boiled over inside, but he had no strength to resist. Every bone was battered, and even breathing was difficult. A patch of purple was beginning to spread from the left side of his rib cage. He spit blood.

"So, what do we start with?" Ashley asked, lifting a pistol with his left hand and cocking the hammer with his thumb. "Fingers? Toes? An ear maybe? Tell me, Devlin. You still feel lucky, alive like you are?"

Willie tried to speak, but his mouth was filling with blood, and he could barely keep his eyes from closing. Spasms of pain choked him.

"Well, Devlin!" Ashley yelled.

It's over, Willie thought. Ambushed, beaten to death by a man I might have killed! It was too absurd to continue. The pistol turned toward his face, and Willie stared fiercely at Shadrack Ashley as if a dying curse might send the killer to an early grave.

"Ears, first," Ashley whispered, laughing. The others echoed their approval. Willie winced.

But before the pistol could fire, a wild cry split the air.

Horses splashed through water, whining as they struggled up the steep embankment. Willie saw Ashley turn his pistol toward an approaching shadow. For one brief instant, from somewhere deep inside, Wil Devlin found the strength to raise a battered right hand. It was just enough to disturb Shad Ashley's aim, and the gun discharged harmlessly toward the clouds as it flew from the outlaw's fingers.

"You!" Ashley cried, slapping Willie to the ground. Then someone or something seemed to lift the one-armed devil from the ground and send him flying. Gunshots and outcries flooded Willie's ears. He saw nothing. Pain overcame every effort to rise.

For a few minutes Willie fought to crack his eyes open. He felt a bullet strike the ground beside his left foot. He waited for the piercing pain that would come from dismembered toes or fingers, from an ear sliced from his head. In the end, though, he felt nothing. A dark, numbing curtain descended on his mind, and there was nothing but an enveloping darkness.

CHAPTER 4

He drifted for a time through a great silver haze. Then he began to recognize things—people and places left behind long ago. It was as if the whole universe suddenly danced by, and Willie reached out and plucked those parts dearest to his heart. He watched as a young Willie Delamer raced spotted ponies through the Brazos shallows. He sat at the dinner table eating his mother's baked chicken and listening to her read stories. He walked with his father on the porch of the old house down by the river, taking to heart wise words now so sorely missed.

He saw the river, the wonderful, rolling Brazos, shimmering in April sunlight. A younger Willie gazed at the bright-faced, yellow-haired girl with the dazzling blue eyes. Ellen. Back then she'd been his Ellen, not married to a Kansas doctor with a family that would never be his. Suddenly the river shrank into a stream. The face of the girl changed. There was Tildy, stretching out her hand, pleading with him.

"Please, Wil, come back to me. We can build a future."

The words took hold, gripped him like powerful hands and pulled him back from the haze, back through the veiled darkness. Pain surged through him. Daggers seemed to pierce his ribs. He coughed, mumbled a cry, then moaned.

For a minute, Willie thought he was still lost in a nightmare. His left eye refused to open, and his ears were filled with echoing thunder. Then his vision began to clear. The pain subsided as he lay still.

Where am I? he wondered. What's happened?

Slowly, calmly, he began to examine his surroundings. He lay on a thick bearskin. His battered body was covered by a pair of soft buffalo hides. He could tell his ribs were bound, and his left leg was splinted. Elsewhere a sticky lotion had been dabbed on bruises too numerous to count.

He sniffed an odor of wood smoke and bear grease. He tried to raise his head, but a hammering pain convinced him to remain still. Even so, he could now identify the tall conical shape of a Plains Indian lodge. Above him, light streamed through the smoke hole.

He lay on the bearskin several minutes before the silver haze recaptured his senses. An hour later he reawakened. This time he stared up at a spry young woman in her late teens dressed in buckskin garb. Her hair was braided Shoshoni fashion.

"Shoshoni?" Willie whispered.

The girl nodded, then smiled. She left only long enough to fetch a bowl of hot broth. This she held to his mouth. Willie sipped slowly. His mouth was sore, and his teeth ached. The broth warmed him, though, and he hungered for more. She brought a second bowl, and a third.

"What happened?" he asked. "Where am I?"

She smiled, touched her forehead, and pulled the buffalo hides away from his chest. He saw more bruises. His left elbow was purple and swollen. The ribs were bound as he suspected, and a deep gash on his left thigh was covered by an herb plaster.

"Ashley did a fair job of it," Willie muttered. Even so, he saw no bullet holes. And he was alive!

"Whose camp is this?" he asked the girl.

She grinned, then began spreading a red-orange paste over the scrapes and scratches that covered Willie's chest, shoulders, and arms. The mixture tingled, then filled his flesh with a cool sensation. A few minutes later the pain faded.

"Thank you," he told her. "What's your name?"

She made a sign like a bird, then pointed to her raven-black hair.

"Black," he said. "Black bird?"

She frowned, then sketched the sharp beak of a crow in the sandy ground beside his bed.

"Black crow?" he asked.

Now she smiled. He took her hand and kissed it lightly. At first she failed to understand. Then she brightened and returned the gesture.

"Thank you, Black Crow, for helping me," Willie told her. "You and your people surely saved my life."

She nodded gravely, then slipped out the oval door. Willie took a shallow breath and closed his eyes. Moments later he was asleep again.

When he next regained consciousness, a tall, wrinkled Shoshoni in his late forties greeted him.

"You are better," he spoke in fine English. "Black Crow Woman has given you broth and tended your wounds. Her medicine has great power. You will grow stronger soon."

"I'm in your debt," Willie said, trying to lift his hand. His shoulders seemed nailed to the ground, though.

"You fell into bad hands," the Indian said, creeping nearer so Willie's outstretched fingers could grasp his own. "These white snakes have no honor."

"I've known snakes," Willie said, fighting to smile. "No snake ever born was half as bad as that bunch. I should've killed 'em when I had the chance."

"You know them?"

"Only their leader by name. Shad Ashley. The others rode down on our camp at Rock Creek. It was clear enough the kind of men they were."

"But you did not kill them?"

"My heart was heavy with killing," Willie explained. "I've seen too much death. I hoped I would be mistaken, that they would go elsewhere."

"Snakes can only crawl a short way," the Shoshoni said, laughing. "But two of them crawl no longer. Raventail has no love of killing, but such men must die."

"You are Raventail?"

"I am," the Shoshoni said proudly. "You are welcome in my camp as all brave warriors are."

"Ten winters back I was in the Bighorn country," Willie explained. "There I heard of a man called Raventail. He was known as a powerful enemy of the Sioux and a man with the best horses in the territory."

Raventail clasped Willie's hand again, and the two quickly took up a discussion of the Bighorns, of rivers and streams where tall elk and grizzlies had been shot. Later they spoke of the fierce Sioux bands that chased the blue-coat soldiers from the forts guarding the Bozeman Trail.

"It was the last of my warrior days," Raventail said sadly. "Now my sons scout for the soldiers at Fort Stambaugh. I am left to guard the old women and the little ones."

"Me, I'd welcome a year or so of peace," Willie declared.

"Peace?" Raventail asked. "Too many snakes here for peace."

Willie nodded his agreement, then lay back and closed his eyes.

"Rest easy, my friend," Raventail whispered. "Grow strong on Black Crow Woman's medicine. One day we will hunt the elk and the grizzly again. For now you must mend."

Willie heard the words, and thereafter he never doubted he would grow stronger. Black Crow Woman returned with broth every few hours. After feeding Willie, she chanted and smeared her herb paste on his wounds. By and by the pain abated. By nightfall of the second day his left eye opened, and he could move his arms slightly.

He was awakened an hour before sundown by the sounds of a horse galloping into the encampment. The Shoshonis howled, and from the subsequent commotion,

Willie suspected a chief might have arrived. Instead Black Crow Woman escorted Gump Barlow into the lodge.

"How'd you get here?" Willie asked.

"Raventail sent a boy to fetch somebody. The boy didn't speak English any too good, but he brought along your shirt. There was enough blood on it to hint of trouble."

"Was Shad Ashley," Willie grumbled. "Got the gold. He's burned Pop's station, and he means to hurt Tildy and Vance. You, too. He's mad at the whole world. You'd better head back and tend . . ."

"I will," Gump assured him. "They'll be fine. From what Raventail's boy said, that bunch of renegades'll be a time mendin'. They'll be walkin' as well."

"Then they're better off than me," Willie complained. "I'm stomped to blazes, Gump. I let 'em take me. It was a pure beauty of an ambush. I'll bet they were waiting days for me to leave Rock Creek."

"Could be," Gump agreed, sitting beside the bearskin bed and inspecting the damage.

"How bad?" Willie asked.

"I'll admit I've seen you in better shape," Gump said, laughing. "That medicine woman, the one that doesn't talk, made the sign for broken ribs. The leg's not broken. You ain't any too pretty to look at, but I'd judge you'll be up and ridin' in a week or so."

"A week at most," Willie insisted. "Won't take Ashley any longer'n that."

"You leave others to worry about him," Gump suggested. "Raventail's sent word to the fort. I passed some soldiers on my way. Mr. Ashley's gone and become a popular fellow hereabouts."

"I'd like to hear he was so popular they hung him up for everyone to see," Willie replied. "Gump, you were right about those four that visited us. They were with Ashley."

"Then we haven't heard the end of this by a long shot," Gump said, frowning. "It's personal."

"With Ashley especially," Willie said, sighing. "I shot him down at Point of Rocks, remember? Well, he wound up losing an arm. Blames me. Lord, his eyes were full of hate. He had some big plans for me when those Shoshonis rode up. I was never so glad to hear a bunch of Indians in all my life."

"I guess not."

Black Crow Woman brought her herbs in then and began chanting. Willie grinned and nodded to Gump. The old man smiled, gave Willie a farewell wave, and promised to visit again on the morrow.

Gump came daily the rest of what proved to be a long week. Willie remained on his back the whole time. Each time he struggled to move, the wound on his thigh would resume bleeding. Worse, the ribs ached severely. Finally, though, he managed to sit up.

"You're better," Gump noted when he saw Willie chewing a strip of dried venison. "Face is almost human again. I brought you some things."

"Oh?" Willie asked.

"Vance found some trousers and a pair of moccasins. Erma Hagen stitched you a shirt."

"And what did you bring?"

"This," Gump said, revealing a Winchester rifle. "Raventail put your pistol belt aside for you, but I figured till you're mended some, you best stick to the rifle. Keep 'em at long range."

"It would seem wise."

"Tildy's been after me to ask when you're up to comin' home."

"Home?"

"To the cabin. She's fixed the place up some for you. Seth and his brothers and sisters found some paint and splashed it on the walls. It's sort of a welcome-home greeting. Guess they miss your huntin'."

"I miss it."

"Well, won't be long once you get up. Soon as those ribs can take some jostlin', I'll have a horse saddled and waitin'."

"Soon," Willie assured his companion. "Soon."

But it was several days yet. Willie sat up some, even took a few steps around the lodge, but the bandaged ribs throbbed at the slightest movement. He sat alone and fretted over Vance and Tildy. At night he imagined Ashley's raiders hitting the cabin, torturing Tildy so that her cries tore through his nightmare and shook him from his slumber.

"Black Crow Woman says you are troubled by bad spirits," Raventail said, sitting beside Willie's bed. "It is this Ashley?"

"Yes," Willie admitted. "I dreamed he killed my friends."

"He is a bad man," Raventail said, frowning heavily. "They kill women, even little ones. The morning they fell upon you, two boys from my camp were killed."

"You sure it was Ashley?" Willie asked.

"I followed his tracks. Those boys . . . one was not yet ten summers old. My grandson, Devlin. The boys had no guns. They could not harm anyone. It wasn't enough to kill them. This Ashley gave them the slow death, with knives. For this reason my people hunt him."

"The soldiers do, too."

"Bluecoats will not find them," Raventail grumbled. "They find no one who doesn't want to be found. Ashley is a devil. For him strong medicine must be used. A Shoshoni will bring his death."

"Or I will," Willie declared.

"What craziness is it that strikes white men to turn their hearts so dark?" Raventail asked. "To kill a boy! To cut him so that his mother would not know him!"

"I've seen it before," Willie said, gripping Raventail's wrist. "Back in Texas I once saw a wounded wolf bite his own paw. It was the only thing close enough to strike! Hate eats a man up. That's what's happened to Shadrack Ashley. He's a wounded grizzly, so to speak."

"The worst kind."

"We best finish him before he eats the whole valley,"

Willie said grimly. "Pity the poor soul who gets in his way."

"Yes," Raventail agreed.

When Willie was finally able to sit a horse, Raventail sent a rider to Rock Creek. Shortly thereafter Vance Bonner rode up leading a saddle pony.

"I expected Gump," Willie declared.

"He thought it best I come," Vance explained. "Said it was on account of my speed on horseback. Truth is we've seen signs of riders at the creek. He worries for Tildy."

"He should," Willie said, walking to where Raventail and Black Crow Woman stood. "You saved my life," he told the Shoshonis, "and I'm ever in your debt. If you need my help, you have it."

Black Crow Woman smiled and drew out a small medicine pouch. She hung it around Willie's neck.

"Strong medicine," Raventail explained. "It will keep you from harm. No dark-eyed one can overcome it."

Willie nodded soberly and kissed the medicine woman's hands. Then he turned and joined Vance. Together they made their way back to Rock Creek.

It was a difficult ride. Willie's battered ribs ached, and his eyes read danger in every shadow. Twice he drew out the Winchester and prepared to fire. Each time a deer darted from view.

"I never saw you this nervous," Vance observed. "You all right, Wil?"

"Do I look it?" Willie asked. "Lord, they nearly killed me, Vance, and they've vowed to do the same to you and Tildy. I take no chances anymore."

"You figure they'll hit the cabin?"

"I sure do. No reason they shouldn't."

"Lot o' open ground there," Vance pointed out. "Man on horseback chargin' up the creek makes a pure wonderful target for that rifle o' yours. This may be easier than you think."

"I wouldn't count too much on that," Willie argued.

When they arrived at Rock Creek, Willie found nothing

had changed. The Hagens and Moffats continued to pan the streambed. Seth waved when Willie rode past, and little Janie Moffat raced over with a handful of flowers. The cabin did indeed have bright yellow walls, and moments after dismounting, Willie was greeted by a gang of grinning neighbors.

"Wish I'd known there was danger on that trail," Ethan Hagen grumbled. "I'd gone with you. They wouldn't take a pair of men so easily."

"Yes, they would have," Willie declared. "They fell on me from all sides. A neat trap it was. Now I know to watch for 'em, though. It won't be so easy to do it again."

The Moffats and Hagens then told how each morning riders appeared at the creek, seemingly scouting the camps.

"I shot one off his horse, but he wasn't hurt so bad he couldn't get away," John Moffat explained. "I don't much like this waitin' game."

"Nor I," Willie added. "But just now I'm not much use on horseback, and only a fool would set out on foot after Shad Ashley."

The others agreed.

When the Hagens and Moffats finally left, Tildy wrapped an arm around Willie's shoulder and led him inside the cabin.

"Still hurts, eh?" she asked.

"Like wildfire," he admitted. "But I've been busted up before. I heal."

"Gump said a young Indian girl tended you."

"Yeah," Willie said, sitting at the edge of his bunk so that Tildy could join him. "Medicine woman. She doesn't talk. Her eyes were bright, but solemn. I saw power there. She made me a sort of charm to ward off evil. I hope it works."

"Me, too," Tildy said, interlacing her fingers with his. "I got a letter from Grandpa. Ashley burned the station house, killed two men."

"Anyone I'd know?"

"Grandpa didn't say. He's shook some. Suggested we head for Cheyenne."

"And?"

"This is home, Willie. We dug up a promising section of quartz yesterday."

"It isn't gold makes you wealthy, you know."

"What does?"

"Belonging. Peace. I don't think we'll find it here."

"Then where, Willie? You don't find peace runnin' away from trouble. It follows by and by."

"Usually," he confessed. "But not always. There's high places in the Wind River Range where nobody'll bother you."

"You mean we just leave Shad Ashley be? He burned Grandpa's station, Wil. He near killed you. Can you forget all that?"

"I'll have to if we're ever to build that future you're always talking about."

"We can do that here, Wil. This cabin can be home if you'll let it be."

"Can it?" Willie wondered for how long. Nothing lasted long, so the Cheyenne were fond of saying. It was all too true. How easily a world was swept away! Death could strike in a flash. And here was Tildy, speaking of the future, when any moment Shad Ashley might ride out of the pines and strike them all down!

"Promise me you'll give it a chance?" Tildy whispered.

"I will," he agreed. But he knew that mattered very little. He touched the painted figure on the medicine pouch lightly, hoping the power inside would ward off Ashley until the ribs had healed, until his eyes were sharp and his hand as quick with a pistol as before.

Lord, give me a little time, he prayed. Just a few weeks. Willie read a similar prayer in Tildy Bonner's eyes, and he gripped her hand tightly. Perhaps, he thought, this once, fate will be kind to Willie Delamer. Just once. He prayed so.

CHAPTER 5

Willie sometimes thought his whole life was born of wind and thunder. His was a trail full of sharp rocks, cut too often by deep gorges and blocked by steep embankments. He could number on one hand the few days of peace that had eased his travail.

"It's the struggles in a man's life makes him strong," his father one told a younger Willie. "What he does with those struggles molds his character . . . and his future."

I've done a poor job of it, Papa, Willie thought. Somewhere way back Willie Delamer had taken the wrong fork in the road, and a world of death and despair had followed. Now it seemed that path once again lay before him.

Shadrack Ashley had likewise taken the fork. The only difference was that Ashley held no regrets. As he rode the hills between Rock Creek and South Pass City, dodging cavalry patrols and Shoshoni warriors, he showed an arrogant defiance of his enemies.

Willie spotted Ashley twice that next week spying on the camps from cover. The one-armed outlaw seemed strangely interested in the Rock Creek camps, Willie thought. There was scarcely enough gold to warrant the risk of a raid. Gump's aim was sharp as ever, and Vance notched the hat of one unwelcome visitor who wandered a bit too close. Raiders would surely pay a high price.

Shad Ashley was no fool. He struck elsewhere. While a mending Wil Devlin kept watch over his companions down at Rock Creek, a dark black plume spiraled skyward from the diggings out at Little Beaver Creek.

"Wil?" Vance called as he discarded his pan and hurried toward the cabin.

"Ashley," Willie growled, spitting a bad taste from his mouth.

John Moffat and Ethan Hagen took note of the smoke as well. Both men ushered their families to safety, then hurried toward the cabin.

"Looks to be trouble to the west," Moffat pointed out. "Maybe we should go have a look."

"Could be Sioux," Hagen added. "The soldiers say there's been a band of 'em in the hills."

"Not Sioux," Gump insisted. "Shad Ashley. Fire's his way of markin' a trail."

Yes, Willie thought. Fire and death.

Minutes later a young rider galloped through the creek, crying out in alarm.

"Raiders!" the boy shouted. "Help!"

Vance started toward the breathless rider, but it was Willie who got there first. After helping the exhausted boy from the saddle, Willie dabbed a kerchief in the creek and washed the young man's smoke-blackened face.

"Ease up a minute," Willie suggested as the others gathered around. "Tell us your name, son. What's happened?"

"I'm Jed Hawkins. I come from the digs over at Little Beaver Creek," the boy said between pants. "A man rode up to us askin' the way to South Pass City. Pa went out to speak with him. Next thing you know, a dozen men are ridin' down on our place, shootin' everybody in sight. Pa fell first. Uncle Jack was caught down at the creek. Little Emily Sides was shot. She only had her sixth birthday last week."

"Was there a one-armed man along?" Willie asked.

"He was the leader," the boy said, glaring at the rising

smoke. "At first a couple of folks shot back. They didn't last long. Wasn't anybody left with a gun. Mostly just women and little kids hidin' in the rocks. Most o' those bandits let up, but that skunk with the one arm said to shoot a few more. Was like drivin' prairie hens out o' the tall grass, it was. They killed my brother Ben! I only got clear myself 'cause I saw a horse and took my chance.

"You got to come back with me. Elsewise they'll kill everybody! Please, come with me now!"

"We'll get our rifles," Hagen said, nervously gazing at Willie.

"And who'll guard this camp?" Willie asked.

"He's right," Vance declared. "You watch your families. Wil and I'll go."

"You?" Gump asked. "You'd hardly know your way there, and Wil can hardly sit a horse."

"I can find my way just fine," Vance insisted. "Who couldn't? There's enough smoke to paint the whole sky black!"

"You up to it, Wil?" Gump asked. "You could stay and watch the camp."

"I'd rather you do that," Willie said, frowning heavily as young Jed's tears began digging white furrows on his grimy cheeks. "Think you can get the horses saddled, Vance?"

"I'll help," Hagen offered, and Vance led the way toward the waiting animals. Willie turned toward the cabin. He'd have the Winchesters loaded and extra shells stuffed in saddlebags by the time the horses were ready. He was still ten feet from the door when Tildy cut him off, though.

"You can't mean to take Vance and that poor boy over there to hunt Ashley?" she cried. "Those ribs want time to heal, Wil."

"We won't find Ashley," Willie grumbled. "Not unless he wants us to. They'll need help tending the wounded, though. And burying the dead."

"You won't be much help with either. Better I should go."

"No!" he shouted. "Tildy, you stay close to Gump. Could be this whole business at Little Beaver's just a way of luring us away from here. It's been done before—to good effect, too."

"Wil, you'll look out for Vance, won't you? He's just seventeen. That's awful young to get killed."

"How old's Jed?" Willie asked, glancing back at the shivering boy. "Fifteen maybe? Seems to me it's the young do much of the dying hereabouts. And the suffering."

She nodded, then followed him inside the cabin. Together they filled the rifle magazines. While Willie stuffed two boxes of shells in one saddlebag, Tildy filled the other with jerked venison. She said nothing, but Willie knew she was preparing herself for the possibility they would be gone several days.

Willie refused to consider that possibility. He had no yearning to set his feet on the bloodstained trail of Shadrack Ashley. His thoughts were haunted by the nightmare vision of Ashley's raiders descending on Rock Creek.

"Wil?" Vance called then.

Willie shook himself out of a stupor and walked to where the two youngsters waited. He handed the saddlebags to Vance and then painfully pulled himself atop his horse. A sour-faced Jed Hawkins led the way toward the diggings two miles westward at Little Beaver Creek.

Jed's tale of fire and murder did not adequately prepare his companions for the scene that met their eyes upon splashing their way across the shallows of Little Beaver Creek. Old mine adits and rough-hewn log cabins lay in smoking ashes. Men lay here and there, their contorted faces attesting to violent death. Women sobbed beside the bodies of fallen husbands. Children tugged at lifeless fingers. Willie nudged his horse to the left to avoid trampling the small figure of a girl. Her left eye had been closed by a single bullet.

Little bundles lay in the rocks. Willie's didn't approach them. He knew what lay beneath the rough woolen blankets, and he shuddered. He had no desire to gaze into the pale, lifeless eyes of another slain child. He had no tears left to shed.

Jed dismounted and hurried over to a pair of thin-faced boys of ten or so. The children instantly wrapped frail arms around the older boy.

"Likely brothers," Vance suggested. "Wil, there must be a dozen dead. A dozen! Look at the little ones! Lord, I promise somebody'll pay for this!"

Other equally angry voices cried for revenge. As miners from the Willow Creek camps arrived, their hardened faces betrayed rare rage.

"Was a one-armed man!" a woman who tearfully cradled a wounded three-year-old cried.

"I recognized his face," a mournful miner added as he dug a grave for his fallen brother. "Was Shadrack Ashley."

"Ashley!" another howled. "Curse him to feel such pain!"

"Who'll ride with me after these animals?" a tall newcomer asked. "Well, who'll go with me to claim just revenge for these murders?"

"I will!" one announced.

"And me!" another and another added.

"How 'bout you?" the tall man asked, turning to Willie. "We know you, don't we? Devlin? You dealt with the Murphys."

"Lead us, Devlin," the company called.

"Wil?" Vance pleaded.

"I've got my own worries," Willie explained.

"You've got more cause then most to want Ashley dead," Vance objected. "He beat you, left you stove in and near dead. You have to go."

"No such thing," Willie said, scowling. "Vance, you don't know this trail like I do. It's full of death. Listen, friends, Ashley isn't apt to wait in some meadow for you to shoot him down. He'll lay ambushes, ride down on you fast and hard. Look around you! This isn't a man who'll leave men to ride homeward. Look to your families. Wait. He'll be back."

"Coward," the tall man grumbled.

"He can't be the one who dropped Doyle Murphy," a woman called.

"Wil?" Vance asked again.

"I won't go," Willie said, sliding off his horse. He reached for a nearby spade, but a girl of fourteen or so snatched it away.

"We'll tend our own," she said, eyeing him furiously. "I can dig this ground. I can't go after those men!"

Willie suddenly found hateful eyes surrounding him. Even Vance appeared hostile.

"I guess that beatin' took more out o' you than I thought," the young man said.

"It's time we headed back," Willie said.

"You go," Vance replied. "I'm not afraid."

Afraid? Willie wondered. Vance didn't know what to fear yet. At seventeen it was hard to understand the darkness that came with killing. It wasn't a thing another could explain, either. It was learned amid echoes of rifle blasts, on trembling knees, holding a father's dying hand.

Willie climbed atop his horse and turned toward Rock Creek.

"You best see him safely home, boy," the miners taunted Vance.

Other words hung in the air like sour apples. As they rode, Willie read suspicion and disappointment in young Vance's eyes. Unspoken words stung worse than bullets.

"I don't understand," Vance said as they crossed the low ridge above Rock Creek. "You're no coward."

"No," Willie mumbled. "I wish I was."

"What?" the young man asked. "I don't understand."

"I know," Willie said, frowning. "I hope you never do."

Vance was more confused than ever. After putting away the horses, he busied himself with chores and left Willie alone. It was, in a way, a silent accusation. Then, at supper, Vance related the whole episode.

"Can't you see, little brother?" Tildy asked. "He was only worried about us."

"No, that wasn't it," Vance insisted. "Was it, Wil? You're afraid."

Willie didn't respond. Instead he left the table and walked out to the creek. There, beside the gentle rolling stream, he tried to erase the nightmare of Little Beaver Creek from his mind. It was impossible. The image remained vivid. And as he recalled the empty eyes of the dead, he saw again battlefields and fallen friends.

"Vance doesn't mean anything," Tildy said, stepping to Willie's side. She gripped his wrist tightly, then continued. "I've seen it before. It's the killing, isn't it? You're tired of it."

"Yes," he admitted. "I told you before how it would be. I can't escape it."

"Grandpa used to say it casts a long shadow."

"The longest," Willie agreed. "Tildy, I've tried to run from it before. I never get far. It'll come down on us like summer hail, out of nowhere. It always does."

"You're safe here," she said, holding him close. "You've got friends. So long as we stick together, nothin' can happen."

"I thought so once," he told her. "Not anymore. I warned you before what happens to folks I care about. It's a dark cloud I bring to others."

"I don't believe that for a moment," she said, laughing. "You're the best kind of man. And I know you'll stand by us no matter what dangers come."

"How can you be so sure?"

"Because I know what's in your heart. And mine. We're two of a kind, Wil Devlin. No trouble's goin' to drive us from each other."

He embraced her, and the warmth of her smile ate away at his gloom. Even so he found little peace that night. In between nightmares, he managed what was, at best, a fretful slumber. Peace remained a distant dream.

CHAPTER 6

Willie awoke to find a morning bright and fine as any to ever grace a Rocky Mountain day. The sun hung in the eastern sky like the biggest golden nugget dug from the South Pass mines. Oceans of blue and yellow wildflowers danced in a gentle breeze. Pairs of cardinals and sparrows turned circles and nipped each other in courtship rituals.

It was good to be alive on such a day. Willie rubbed the soreness from his scarred thigh and breathed deeply for the first time since cracking his ribs. For a brief moment Little Beaver Creek was forgotten. Shad Ashley seemed a world away. The elder Moffat boys, Clark and Jake, chased their little brother and sister through the creek. A few yards downstream Seth Hagen plucked trout from the water. Tildy strung laundry on her makeshift line. Even old Gump seemed caught by the mood. He hummed a jaunty melody as he sifted sand in his tin pan.

Only Vance was sour. The seventeen-year-old's scowl sent sharp darts into Willie's heart. Understanding wasn't forthcoming as of yet. Neither was forgiveness.

"Give him time," Tildy suggested as Willie helped her hang the wash.

"Yes, time," Willie agreed, knowing all the while how fate had a way of hurrying things along.

The first sign of trouble came an hour later. It was Seth

Hagen who spotted the rider. A burly man wrapped in a buffalo cloak in spite of the warm weather emerged from the distant pines atop a speckled mare. The long barrel of a Sharps rifle protruded from the cloak.

"Pa!" Seth called.

The shout carried traces of alarm, and Willie instantly located the youngster. Following Seth's pointing finger, Willie also detected the intruder.

"Tildy, get inside," Willie commanded as he fetched his rifle and headed for the creek. As he went, he waved the Moffat girls out of the water and on toward their camp. Vance set aside his pan, and Gump splashed his way to the bank.

"Trouble?" the old-timer asked.

"See for yourself," Willie answered, pointing out a pair of riders closing in from the east. Another now splashed into the creek from the north. Two more appeared on a hillside southwest of the Moffats and Hagens.

"I'll take the cabin," Gump said, grabbing his rifle.

"Go with him," Willie told Vance.

The young man shook his head and huddled behind a slag heap. Willie frowned, but he didn't argue. Instead he hurried to a boulder lying halfway between the cabin and the creek. It offered a good vantage point for seeing the northern end of the creek and its approaches. If the Moffats and Hagens held the south, the raiders had a poor chance of success.

Had Shad Ashley been a man prone to caution, he might never have fired a shot at the Rock Creek camps. That would have suited Willie fine. But Ashley and three others charged the little canvas hovel of Ethan Hagen with reckless abandon. One raider fell, but the surviving trio tore into the camp, shooting wildly and shouting like devils escaped from hell.

"Lord!" Vance cried in disbelief as a flurry of gunfire erupted. A gray cloud of dust and powder smoke devoured canvas and wagons. Small figures darted for safety as pistols sent fiery daggers their way. Vance raced to Willie's side as rifle bullets showered the slag heap.

"What'll we do?" the youngster called.

Willie swallowed, tightened his gun belt, and ran his hand along the cold barrel of his rifle. Something within him froze his hands. He seemed unable to move, to shoot, to think.

"Wil?" Vance asked. "Comin'?"

The boy rested his weight on his heels, preparing like a perched cougar to spring forward. Better than a hundred yards of open ground separated the boulder from the neighboring camp. It would be a blind, foolhardy charge, little better than rushing naked up a slope against a battery of cannon.

Willie remembered such charges. He recalled wading past the fallen bodies of friends as rifle volleys swept a hillside clean of gray-clad boys whose courageous folly left the ranks thin and the camps silent.

"Well?" Vance asked.

"It's sure death," Willie pointed out. "We'd be better advised circling around, hitting 'em from the rear."

"And who's goin' to be left alive down there then?" Vance cried. "Suit yourself, but I'm goin'."

Willie reached out for the youngster, but Vance slapped the hand aside. By now horsemen encircled the tormented camp, blazing away from short range. Vance leaped out and raced onward. Willie took a deep breath and followed.

Neither of them gave much thought to their charge beforehand, and there was no chance now. Willie left his feet to choose their own course. He kept himself as low to the ground as possible and hoped the raiders had poor aim. He dared not fire his own rifle with Vance up ahead.

The boy ran like a spring antelope, bounding over rocks and leaping across ditches. Vance fired as he came, upsetting the raiders' horses and causing their returning shots to be wild and off the mark. Then a bearded outlaw jumped clear of his frantic pony and turned a pistol toward the onrushing youngster.

"No!" Willie yelled, halting and shouldering his Winchester. His arms steadied the rifle, and his finger squeezed the trigger. The bearded outlaw's shoulder flew back, and the pistol discharged harmlessly. Vance finished the raider himself with a single rifle shot from close range.

Willie dove for the cover of the creek bank as an avalanche of lead suddenly fell upon him. Bullets tore slices from rock or threw up little clouds of sand. He cowered behind the bank and tried to locate a target. Raiders seemed everywhere, but no sooner did Willie fix one in his sights than the scoundrel vanished.

"Where are you, Devlin?" Shad Ashley shouted. "Let's have it done with!"

Ashley's face emerged for a single moment from the thick black smoke bellowing out of the Moffat wagon. Willie took aim, but little Peter Hagen darted out, blocking the shot.

"Vance, to your left!" Willie shouted. Vance reached out and grabbed the scampering five-year-old seconds before a rifle bullet sliced through the air behind him.

Willie hardly caught his breath before he heard something splash into the creek behind him. He turned his rifle and only just managed to keep from shooting Seth Hagen. The boy burrowed his way into the bank at Willie's side as a horseman galloped upstream.

"Where'd you get to, boy?" the rider hollered. "Don't make it tough. Stand up, and I'll make it quick like I did for your old man."

Seth shuddered, and Willie bit his lip. A new fire burned inside him, and he crawled past Seth so as to shield the boy from his tormentor. The grinning raider waved a rifle and searched out the cowering boy. Willie aimed and fired in the same motion. The raider's face filled with surprise as a patch of red spread across his shirt. The outlaw tumbled from the saddle and splashed into Rock Creek.

Seth dashed over and rescued the killer's discarded rifle from the bank. Moments later Seth was firing at the encircling gunmen.

They learn quickly, Willie thought as he slipped past Seth and prepared to dash closer. He sprang to his feet and rushed onward, covering fifteen yards before diving face first into a tangle of willow saplings. He landed on his chest, and pain shot through his injured ribs. For a moment he couldn't breathe.

When he recovered, he found the raiders had moved back to the cover of the unburned Hagen wagon. The powder smoke was fading, and Willie was able to detect Ethan Hagen's corpse lying a few feet from the campfire. A small child rested nearby. Clarice Moffat sat in a rocking chair that swayed in the wind. She still held embroidery in her hands. Her eyes were closed, though, and Willie knew she was dead.

In truth, the only sign of life was Seth, blazing away with his rifle. Vance and Peter were likely off to the right somewhere if the raiders hadn't killed them.

"And me?" Willie muttered. "I'm all alone out here."

He'd been there before, of course. He recalled vividly being ambushed down on the Purgatory, in another gold camp, by men as hate-filled and vicious as Shad Ashley. Back then Willie'd felt in command, confident. He wasn't at all sure of himself now. He hadn't even spied a target.

Well, I ought to be dead already, he told himself. Ashley might have finished me the first time, or the Murphys might have aimed a bit better. I've been shot so many times . . .

He swept it all out of his mind. He could smell the powder and the stench of burning leather. The flaming Moffat wagon up ahead seemed to taunt him. There were hopes and dreams in there, all blazing away.

"Just like your dreams, Willie," a voice seemed to whisper. "Soon you'll lie up there, bleeding and alone."

"No!" Willie shouted.

His cry alerted the raiders, and a pair of them charged toward the creek. Willie plucked the first from his saddle, and the second turned and rode wildly out into the safety of the distant pines.

"Kelly?" Ashley howled. No one answered, though. For the first time the tide seemed to turn. The horsemen who had been lurking upstream moved cautiously back into the cover of the trees. The shooting abated. Finally Willie spotted a strip of red cloth tied to a small twig waving from a pile of rocks over on his right. Vance wore a red shirt like that, and the young man's face glanced up moments later.

So, I'm not alone after all, Willie thought. Slowly, cautiously, he crawled on his belly to the rocks. He remained alert for any sign of the outlaws, but he managed to elude their attention and reach Vance safely. Tiny Peter Hagen huddled there as well.

"I'm down to my last two shells," Vance said as Willie rested a nervous hand on the boy's shoulder. "Didn't think to start out with a full magazine. Guess I've done smarter things than charge up here."

"I'd say so," Willie said, reaching into his pocket and drawing out a handful of shells. As Vance reloaded, Willie did likewise. The air was strangely quiet. Echoes of gunshots rang through Willie's ears, but his eyes blinked away exhaustion and studied the ground ahead.

Two horses prowled around the remaining wagon. A rifle barrel kept watch from behind a large crate.

"I'd guess two, maybe three over there," Willie told Vance. The young man nodded, then pointed out a shadow on the slope to the right.

"There's one or more on horseback there."

"One's down at the creek," Peter whimpered.

"So is Seth," Willie said, touching the child lightly on the ear. "Gump's back of that. It's the ones up ahead we have to watch."

"Another charge?" Vance asked.

"Just now I've managed to avoid putting any new holes in my hide," Willie responded. "I'd like to keep it that way. As for you, all the luck a man's entitled to's come your way this morning. I wouldn't hold out hope for much more."

"Then what?" Vance asked.

"We go slow, ease our way around the right where you saw those shadows. Anybody pops out, you be ready."

"You're not leavin' me, are you?" Peter whined.

"You just dig yourself in, son," Willie told the five-year-old. "We'll have this business concluded 'fore long now."

Peter nodded and squeezed his small frame between two boulders. Willie waved Vance along, and the two of them crept from the rocks and closed on the trees up ahead. Two horsemen spotted them and shouted a challenge.

"That you, Shad?" the first asked.

Willie answered with his Winchester, and the raiders beat a hasty retreat.

"Well?" Vance asked, pointing toward the apparently deserted Hagen wagon.

Only ashes remained of the Moffat wagon. What stores and belongings weren't burned had been flung around like scattered chaff. There was no way to close on the surviving wagon from cover. Only blackened earth lay ahead.

"I know they're up there," Vance whispered. "I don't see 'em, but I know they're there."

Willie nodded his agreement, then set aside his rifle. A pistol was the proper tool for close-in fighting.

"Cover me," Willie said, preparing himself for a second charge.

"You cover me," Vance suggested. "I run a whole lot faster than you."

"And what'll you do when you get there?" Willie asked. "You won't get any second shots. You ever kill a man from two feet away? Ever feel his breath on you when you shot him? This is no job for you, Vance Bonner."

"I've been steady enough, haven't I?"

"Has nothing to do with it," Willie said, gazing sternly at his young friend. "It's a dark-hearted devil's needed for this, and I'm just the man to do it."

Willie then jumped out into the open and raced toward the wagon. His legs ached, and his chest felt on fire. Even so, when the first outlaw jumped up, Willie shot the man in the head.

"Taft?" Ashley screamed, firing wildly from the corner of the wagon. Willie fired, too, and Shadrack Ashley dropped to one knee.

"Shad's down!" a raider howled.

Immediately the remaining horsemen dashed toward their horses and raced away. All but one, that is. The remaining outlaw leaped from the wagon and crashed onto Willie's back, sending him rolling hard against the rocky ground. The outlaw raised a boot to kick Willie's battered ribs, but Willie swung the barrel of his pistol and smashed it against the outlaw's kneecap. The raider cried out in pain and limped away. Willie turned his pistol toward the fleeing outlaw, but he was distracted by a sudden shout.

"Wil, look out!" Vance cried.

Willie rolled over, avoiding a pair of hastily fired pistol shots. He then edged over to the wagon as a third shot tore a spoke from one of the rear wheels. The fleeing raider meanwhile made good his escape.

"To your left!" Vance shouted, and Willie fired. His bullet struck the toe of a limping Shad Ashley's boot. The outlaw grinned and coldly answered Willie's shot. Ashley's bullet clipped Willie's left arm, opening a healthy gash but leaving him otherwise unhurt.

"Wil?" Vance called, rushing forward.

Ashley then turned and fired a single shot into the young man. Vance stumbled, dragging himself a few feet further before the life seemed to rush out of him. His hand reached toward the wagon and went limp.

Willie jumped out and rapidly fired the remaining chambers of his pistol. Shad Ashley had vanished, though. A taunting laugh marked his passage.

"Next time, Devlin, I'll finish the job!" the outlaw promised as his horse splashed into Rock Creek. "Next time!"

Willie paid little attention. He tied a kerchief over his bleeding arm and drew Vance closer.

"He got away," the young man mumbled. "Tildy? Where's Tildy?"

"Safe in the cabin," Willie assured his young friend as he fought to stop the blood rushing from a hole in the boy's side.

"Wil, I'm scared," Vance muttered.

"You'll be fine," Willie said, tearing off his shirt and using it like a bandage to retard the bleeding. "I've mended many a man in my time."

"It's my fault," Vance whimpered, spitting blood. "I was watchin' him. I only looked away . . . only a second . . . and . . ."

"Hush," Willie commanded. "You'll be fine. Just let me get you back to the cabin."

"Tildy?"

"She's waiting for you," Willie assured the boy. "Just another minute or so, and you'll see for yourself."

Vance gazed up with glazed eyes, then smiled faintly. Willie lifted the young man onto one shoulder and started toward the cabin. Strange how light Vance felt just then. He was solid as granite and wound tight as a spring. At that moment there seemed nothing to him at all.

"You'll be fine," Willie whispered as he continued on toward the cabin. "We'll find a big buck, cook up some venison steaks to help you get your strength back. In a week you'll be chasing me through Rock Creek."

Over and over Willie said it, even though he felt Vance's moist shoulder against his own bare chest.

"Tildy! Gump!" Willie called as he stumbled along.

Seth Hagen and little Peter appeared from where they had been hiding. Their sad eyes stared silently as Willie trudged past. John Moffat and his two youngest emerged as well.

Willie said nothing to any of them. His face was streaked with sweat. He met Gump and Tildy at the cabin, and they helped him ease Vance onto a waiting bed.

"Tildy?" the wounded boy called as she began bathing the wound.

"Rest easy, little brother," she said, trembling as she washed away the blood from the young man's sunken chest.

"Wil?" Vance called next.

"You'll be all right," Willie said, gripping Vance's cool hand tightly. "Just rest."

Vance nodded, then slowly closed his eyes. A grim silence then settled over the cabin. Willie unbuckled his belt and flung his pistol angrily against the wall.

Lord, he silently prayed, *don't take this one. He's needed.*

It was a prayer spoken too often before. And rarely answered.

CHAPTER 7

Willie helped Tildy bind the wound. At first glance it didn't appear to be too bad. There was a fearful lot of blood, but the bullet had passed cleanly through Vance's upper left side.

"No bullet to cut out," Tildy observed. "Thank God for that."

Gump was worried, though. The old-timer didn't say anything, but Willie watched him pace back and forth while Tildy plugged the twin holes.

"Never good to see a man hit in the chest or the belly," Gump told Willie when they stepped outside to see what could be done for the others. "You know any medicine chants from your Comanche days, best use 'em."

Willie had already placed the Shoshoni pouch by Vance's side, hoping any healing powers possessed by the Shoshoni marking might take effect.

"He's young," Willie pointed out. "And it's not even summer. Winter's a time for dying. The young should mend this time of year."

"I seen 'em die in May, too," Gump grumbled. "My fault for allowin' that boy to come along."

"You're forgetting Ashley hit the station, too," Willie said, frowning. "You can't shield 'em, Gump. Fate does as she pleases. You know that."

"I do," the old man admitted. "But I'd have it different."

"Me, too," Willie confessed.

They soon had other worries, though, and Willie spoke no more of Vance. The young man wasn't far from his thoughts, but there was no time to voice his concern. Seth Hagen huddled with his mother and little Peter. Eleven-year-old Althea tended her battered brother Alex. Molly and Myrtle, the younger girls, sat quietly beside the corpse of their father.

The Moffats were hit even worse. John and his eldest, Cathleen, dug a grave for Clarice. Clark and Jake, the older boys, did their best to salvage a few belongings from the wreck of the camp. Little June and her brother Stuart cowered in the bed of the wagon. Their sister Janie lay where she fell.

"Eight years old," John said, noticing Willie had bent down to carry the girl out of the bright sunlight. "Shot down while she was readin' her prayer book."

"Pa?" Cathleen asked as her father flung his spade aside.

"What's the sense of such a thing happenin'?" Moffat asked. "Why'd they come? I scarce had fifty dollars worth of gold, and they didn't get that. I'd handed it over easy enough. There was no call to ride down on us like this!"

Willie didn't answer straightaway. Instead he carried little Janie over to a nearby willow and lay her beneath the shade. Her eyes were wide open, seemingly questioning what had befallen her. Willie remembered how the girl had brought him flowers.

"She had the sweetest voice imaginable," Willie told her father. "I loved to listen to her in the evening down by the creek."

"You'd think an angel dropped down for a visit," Moffat said, smiling in a far-off way.

"Ma favored her," Cathleen added. "Tried not to, but Janie was her favorite."

"We didn't mind," Clark said, turning toward his dead

sister. "She got after you some, but she could cook good flapjacks, and she wasn't a bad checker player."

"Now she's dead," Moffat said bitterly. "For what? A bit of gold? The world's gone crazy."

"Not the world," Willie argued as he stepped over to little Alex Hagen. "Shadrack Ashley."

"I swear he'll pay for what he's done!" Moffat vowed.

"No one can ever do that," Erma Hagen objected. "My Ethan's worth more than a hundred murderin' thieves!"

"Another man's death won't bring back those taken from us," Willie said, lightly touching Alex's chest. "Some who did this are already dead," Willie went on, pointing to the bodies of the dead outlaws scattered around the camp and across the creek. "But Ashley warrants stopping."

"He'll be stopped," Seth declared. "He's killed Pa. He ought to hang high for that. I'll ride and tell the soldiers."

"You'd best help your ma just now," Willie suggested. "You're the eldest. She'll need you."

Seth nodded sadly, and Willie turned his attention to Alex. The boy's face was scraped and bloodied, and a knife had taken a fair-sized slice out of his left thigh.

"Hurt some, eh?" Willie whispered.

Alex bobbed his head slightly, and Willie opened his shirt to show the faint red marks left by a Yank cavalry saber ten years before.

"I looked like a stuck pig," Willie declared. "But scars heal, and so do boys."

"They tossed him about somethin' fearful," Althea explained. "Was right after they shot Janie."

"They shot at me, too," Alex said, shuddering. "Missed."

"Boys are awful hard to hit," Althea said, grinning. "They squirm so you can't clip their hair, and they vex you so you want to tear your hair out. Even so, I guess I'll have to see this one mended."

"She will, too," Willie said, rubbing a tear from the boy's cheek. "There's not too much of you, Alex, but I'd judge what's there is prime enough to be from Texas."

"You from Texas, Mr. Devlin?" Seth asked. "I got an uncle out there."

"Fair place, Texas," Willie told them. "Great rolling rivers, and plains that stretch halfway to next week."

"Tell us about it," Alex pleaded.

"On toward nightfall," Willie promised. "Just now I've got somebody I need to look in on. Maybe Gump'll stay and tell you about his days on the Green River."

"Mr. Gump?" Seth asked.

Gump appeared reluctant to stay behind, but Willie silently pleaded with the old-timer.

"I wasn't much bigger'n young Seth here," Gump began, turning a barrel on its end and sitting on it.

Willie left Gump to entertain the children while John Moffat and Cathleen finished digging. Later Willie would help Seth dig a trench for Ethan. Another grave would be needed for the outlaws. Just now Willie felt the need to see Vance.

The young man was sitting up in his bed when Willie reentered the cabin. Vance's face was pale from loss of blood, and his fingers felt cold.

"You look like somebody's taken a stick to you, Vance," Willie noted. "A big stick!"

"Big rifle," Vance said, trying to grin.

"Got yourself shot up some, eh?"

"I been shot before," the boy reminded Willie. "Worse, too."

"Don't see how it could be much worse," Willie said, sitting on the edge of the bed and fighting the worry off his face. "Got all your fingers and ears, though. That's what Ashley mainly likes to shoot."

"Well, I heard he prefers women and little kids," Vance said, nodding toward the open door. "I saw Miz Moffat and little Janie. Anybody else?"

"Ethan Hagen," Willie said solemnly. "Young Alex was roughed up some, but he's strong."

"So am I," Vance insisted. "Wait and see if I'm not up and dancin' 'fore you are, Wil Devlin."

"Well, if you are, I hope you can do a better job of it than me. I near trampled the last girl I led across a dance floor, and I was a pure embarrassment to my regiment in Richmond."

"I'll bet you were the most dashing soldier in the room," Tildy said, laughing. "Charmed all those city girls out of their petticoats."

"No, I smelled of horses and gunpowder," Willie explained. "I was too bowlegged for their taste, and my trousers were patched. They didn't have much use for me. I was more at home with the Comanches."

"Did you dance with them?" Vance asked.

"Once, a long time back," Willie recounted. "Wasn't much good at that, either."

"Tildy can teach you. She's fair."

Vance started to speak more, but he coughed violently. Tildy put a kerchief to his mouth, and he spit blood into it.

Lung shot, Willie thought. Now that he looked, he noticed how Vance's left side seemed caved in. The boy was lung shot and was likely bleeding inside. Back in Willie's soldier days, that had always been a death sentence. But Vance was young and strong, well fed, and determined to recover.

"Doesn't sound so good, does it?" Vance asked, trying to conceal the bloodstained kerchief. "Doesn't feel any better."

"Maybe you'd be more comfortable lying down," Tildy said.

"I got plenty o' time for that later," Vance said soberly. "I got things to say first."

"Nothing that won't wait," Willie argued.

"Lots that won't," Vance insisted. "Tildy, you figure maybe you could get some air? Just a minute or so."

"I'm not leavin' you," she told him.

"Please?" Vance begged.

"Just a minute then. I'll be just outside. You need anything, holler."

"Wil here'll hold my hand," Vance said, forcing a smile

on his face. "You been a doc, Wil? Been almost everything else, to hear tell."

"Only when I was all there was," Willie explained as Tildy slipped past. "Not much of a bullet digger, I confess."

"She gone?" Vance whispered.

"In the doorway," Willie answered. "What've you got to say to me that she can't hear? We're close to family, Vance."

"I know that," he said, wincing as a spasm of pain wound its way through his chest. "This is personal, though. I got to say it now, too, 'cause I don't know I'll have another chance."

"You'll have a lifetime of chances."

"Will I? You say what you want, but I know what it means when a man coughs blood. Wil, I done you wrong lately."

"Wrong? You? Vance, you've been like a brother to me since the first night I met you. You could never wrong me."

"I did. I thought you were afraid to go after Ashley with those miners. I should've known better. I saw you fight off the Murphys . . . twice. There never was a man for facin' up to a fight like you. I was all wrong. You're no coward."

"That's just a word, Vance. I never took any of that to heart."

"Didn't you? I saw your face when I stared at you."

"It's all forgotten."

"And forgiven?"

"Sure. Now you rest easy and mend."

"Wil, I been so stupid. If I'd done like you said, I'd never gotten shot."

"Or if I'd finished Ashley right off."

"I had a gun, too. My mistake. I've made a lot of 'em lately."

"You're entitled. It goes with being young."

"Pop used to say you don't get many chances to be this wrong."

"A wise man, your grandpa," Willie observed.

Vance coughed again, hard, so that his whole body shook. Again he spit blood. This time his chest seemed to cave in. His breathing became labored. Tildy rushed in and knelt beside her brother.

"I don't guess I'll see another snow," Vance whispered. "I'll miss that. We never got to St. Louis, either, did we, Sis? I sure did want to ride one of those paddle wheelers Pop used to talk about. Do that for me, will you, Tildy?"

"You do it for yourself, Vance Bonner," she said, pretending anger. Tears fell down her hardened cheeks, though.

"I was wonderin' if maybe you could put me up high someplace, so maybe I could see the pass. That way I could watch all the people comin' past."

"Stop it, Vance," Tildy pleaded.

"You'll do it, won't you, Wil?" the boy asked.

"Sure," Willie agreed. "If that's how you want it."

"Stop talkin' like you're dyin'!" Tildy shouted. "I won't have it."

"It's all right, Sis." Vance said, taking her hand. "I'm not scared, you know. I never liked it that much around here anyway. Gump says when a spirit leaves, it dances on the clouds. I always thought that's not so bad. I'll miss you some, and I did want to ride that paddle wheeler, but cloud dancin' won't be so bad."

Gump slipped inside the room. He nodded gravely toward Vance, but the old man showed no other emotion. For several minutes Vance spoke about the mountains, about friends and family, about his dreams.

"It's awful dark," he finally said. "I can see the evenin' star. Out early, isn't it?"

"Sure is," Willie said, frowning. It was scarcely past noon, and the sun blazed down in all its glory.

"I'll be up there dancin' those clouds, Gump," Vance whispered. "Dancin' round and round like a cyclone. It's awful cold, though. I must've lost my coat. Tildy? Tildy, hold my hand."

She gripped it tightly, but he didn't seem to notice. Instead his eyes grew wide, and he coughed again. Then his chest rose and fell a final time.

"Vance?" Tildy called. "Don't leave me, Vance!"

She pulled his limp body to her and sobbed. Willie stepped back and fought to control his own sadness.

"I promised to put him up high," Willie told Gump. "Know a good place?"

"We'll find one," Gump promised. "Well clear o' the digs so he'll only see the land as God molded it."

"Sure," Willie agreed.

"I figure just now maybe we ought to leave 'em alone," Gump said, nodding toward Tildy.

"There're graves need digging," Willie said, swallowing a tear. "And folks who could use some looking after."

"Wil?" Tildy called as he stepped to the door.

"Yes," he answered, turning back toward her.

"Will you make him a box? He had awful nightmares about worms gettin' to Ma and Pa."

"Worms like wood better'n canvas," Gump argued.

"Please?" she asked. "And if Erma Hagen's up to it, I'd appreciate her readin' somethin' from her Bible."

"I'm sure she'd be happy to do it," Willie assured Tildy. "Be back when I finish with the graves."

"Vance wanted to rest high," she said, rubbing her eyes dry. "So he could see all the people passin' by."

"He can see 'em already," Willie declared. "Up on his cloud."

"Yes," she said, trying unsuccessfully to force a smile onto her face.

Willie devoted those next two hours to scratching out a grave for Ethan Hagen out of the rocky ground. The outlaws were buried in a shallow, unmarked grave on the far side of the creek.

"Shouldn't we mark it?" Althea Hagen asked.

"Why?" Willie asked. "What would you write? Thieves? Killers? I don't know their names. Those men are sure to face a terrible judgment now, though."

"He's right," John Moffat agreed. "Let the earth swallow their bones. Their souls are already afire."

"Amen," Erma Hagen added.

Toward dusk the following day, Vance Bonner was laid to rest a quarter-mile away, atop a pine-studded ridge. Erma Hagen read words of comfort, and Tildy spoke of her wiry brother, recalling the good and the bad that life had brought them.

"Lord, hold him near," Erma prayed aloud. "He was a fine boy who would've made a good man."

"He was a good man already," Willie added. "Maybe not in the eyes of strangers, but he shouldered his burdens, and he never backed away from a friend."

"May that be said of us all," John Moffat added.

Later, when Tildy had shed her tears and said her prayers, Willie led her to the creek.

"Seems awful quiet tonight," she whispered.

"I miss Janie's singing," Willie confessed. "And Vance's pranks."

"You were proud of him, weren't you? It meant a lot to him that you fought at his side."

"I was proud of him for working the creek, too," Willie told her. "I'd been happier if he'd stayed behind."

"That's not your fault," Tildy insisted. "He was my responsibility. I should've stopped him."

"Wasn't to be," Willie grumbled. "Couldn't either of us do that."

"I never tried," she said, sobbing. "I hurried him. He was just a little boy!"

"Seventeen," Willie reminded her. "I've known plenty of boys never got that old. I was fifteen when I shouldered a rifle and signed the muster book. At seventeen I was leading men in battle. Wasn't you hurried him, Tildy. Life does that. You were his sister, and you had to leave him room to grow into a man."

"He grew fine," she said, shivering. "Now he's dead. God, I miss him. I hurt worse than I could ever've imagined."

"I know," he said, holding her tightly. "I feel the loss, too."

"You? You're hard as a rock, Wil Devlin. Nothin' shakes you."

"I hide it fair," he told her. "I do my crying inside, where it hurts worst of all. I don't shed tears, Tildy. I grow bitter."

"You think Gump's right about dancin' on clouds?"

"I'd guess Vance's likely riding the moon to tomorrow," Willie told her. "He's up there somewhere, all right, likely laughing up a storm."

"Probably," she agreed.

They walked silently back and forth along the creek until their legs would carry them no more. Then they returned to the cabin and took to their beds. Willie listened to the haunting silence that filled the cabin, broken only by Tildy's muffled sobs. He gazed at the empty bed across the room and felt his heart quiver. Once again death had sought him out. Its cold fingers had reached out to snatch the best from a heartless world. Willie bit his lip and swallowed the bitterness.

CHAPTER 8

Willie awoke to the sound of bacon frying in Tildy's skillet. For a moment he forgot about the smoke and fire that had visited Rock Creek that previous day. He yawned away his fatigue and sat up. His ribs gave him a fiery twinge, though, and he found himself staring at Vance's empty bed. It all came back to him.

Outside, the sun was far too bright. The air was too fresh and alive. The earth itself should have been mourning. Instead robins and cardinals sang.

"Mornin', Wil," Gump said from the far corner of the room. The old-timer was resting rifles and a shotgun against the wall. A world of pain was etched in Gump's ancient face.

"Morning," Willie replied, turning to Tildy. She said nothing as she drew slices of bacon from the skillet. She spooned flapjack batter into the grease and watched it sizzle.

Willie stared down at his bandaged midsection, then wrapped a flannel shirt around his shoulders. He pulled on a pair of trousers and headed outside. Seth Hagen and the Moffat boys were down at the creek fetching water. Their sisters huddled with Erma Hagen around a campfire. John Moffat stood watch over them all with a rifle.

Willie read the mixture of grief and fear in the eyes of

his neighbors. That was the worst thing about the raid. It chased away childhood, leaving only doubt and suspicion. He stepped to the woodpile and fingered the cold steel bit of an ax. Another day he would have cut firewood for the stove. Now he merely turned and reentered the cabin.

"Flapjacks and bacon for breakfast," Gump announced. The old man tried to smile, but his tired eyes betrayed the sadness that lay beneath. Willie nodded somberly and sat at the table.

He couldn't help recalling how Vance used to enjoy flipping flapjacks up in the air, then catching them in the skillet. Most days the youngster could turn them almost magically. Once, though, he'd managed to catch the half-cooked flapjack on his nose. As Vance scraped the goo from his face, Willie'd laughed heartily.

"Your face wasn't so ugly you had to hide it, boy," Gump had remarked.

Willie smiled as he remembered. The smile soon faded, though, and he barely touched his breakfast. His insides were hollow in a way that bacon and flapjacks would not, could not, fill.

Tildy noticed. She had no words of comfort to offer, but afterward, when Willie took Vance's place drying the plates she washed down at the creek, she spoke of her own feelings.

"I remember when Ma and Pa died," Tildy said as she passed Willie the last plate and started on the cups. "I felt my heart was torn in two. I just thought I knew pain, though. Lord, Wil, he was just seventeen."

"Not even full grown," Willie whispered as he rubbed the plate dry. "Seems the world hurries 'em sometimes."

"Or we do," Tildy muttered.

"Oh, I think Vance mainly hurried himself," Willie said, sighing as he recalled the boy eagerly charging after Ashley's raiders. "Boys have a way of doing that sometimes."

"And death's out there waitin'."

"Always," Willie agreed. "Isn't anything you can do

about it. That's what's hard, isn't it? Knowing there's nothing you can do."

She didn't answer at first. Instead she rinsed the rest of the cups and waited for Willie to dry them. It was only after they had started back toward the cabin that she spoke.

"I rocked him on my knee the night Ma died," she explained. "He was so little then. All that year it seemed one fever or another would take him. Then we outlasted the Sioux, survived the Murphy brothers, and I thought the worst had passed."

"That's how it was for me, too," Willie said, leaning against the door. "I fought four long years back East hoping to get back home. Then when I got back, I found it wasn't home at all. Everything had changed, and there was no place for me there.

"Out here it doesn't seem like there's a place for anybody," Willie added. "Just ridges ready to be graveyards."

Tildy turned away to hide her tears. Willie frowned and headed for the old leather chest that held the mining gear.

"Gump?" Willie asked as he drew out the first of the tin pans.

Gump sat in the far corner of the cabin. He had one of the Winchesters broken apart and was cleaning the barrel. He glanced up a minute, shook his head, and resumed his labors.

"Tildy?" Willie asked, handing her a pan. "It's time we got down to the creek, started our work."

"Work?" she asked, turning and angrily throwing the pan against the wall. The clanging sound startled them all, and for a moment an awkward silence filled the place. Finally Tildy wiped her eyes and stared at Vance's empty bed.

"What does it matter?" she asked. "Who cares if we find an ocean of dust? Vance is dead! Tomorrow Ashley may ride down and finish the rest of us."

"No he won't," Gump declared. "He'll be dead."

"Will he?" Tildy asked, turning to Willie. "Well?"

Willie stepped to the door, dragging the pans along with

him. He wanted to say something, but he couldn't stand the fiery plea in her eyes. Instead he continued along to the creek, kicked off his boots, rolled up his trouser legs, and began working the stream.

He hoped the work would ease some of the pain or at least distract him. It did neither. He sifted sand for close to an hour before he even located one flake. A minute later he heard someone splash into the creek downstream. He discarded the pan, drew his pistol, and turned in that direction.

"It's just me, Mr. Devlin!" Seth Hagen called, lifting his hands. "I mean you no harm."

"I know," Willie said, replacing his pistol in its holster and wading over to rescue his drifting pan. "Shouldn't come up on a man from behind after what's happened lately. None too safe."

"No, I guess not," Seth agreed.

"Can't be too careful, you know."

"Sure," Seth said, pointing to where his horse was tethered. A rifle protruded from a saddle scabbard. Provisions were tied behind the saddle.

"Going someplace?" Willie asked.

"Thought to," the thirteen-year-old explained. "Ma was up most of the night. She tried not to let on, but I could tell she'd been cryin'. The little ones, too. Only Althea was really sleepin'. Nothin' shakes her. Alex—well, he's gettin' some better, but he's in no shape to hunt outlaws."

"That what you have in mind?"

"Somebody's got to, Mr. Devlin. Can't let 'em kill anybody else. You figure maybe the two of us could track 'em, maybe . . ."

"Maybe what?" Willie asked. "Kill 'em? You think you've got a murderer's heart, Seth?"

"I buried Pa yesterday," Seth said, grinding his teeth. "I could kill the man that did it. Yes, sir."

"I buried somebody myself yesterday," Willie muttered. "Vance was in too much of a hurry to get killed. Do yourself a favor, son. Give yourself time."

"You'd find me up to the ride, Mr. Devlin. I got a fair eye for shootin', and my grandpa taught me to follow a trail."

"Follow the one that takes you back to your family," Willie advised. "Your ma's had enough grief, and she'll need your help."

"They'll come back, you know."

"Then they'll die!" Willie said, angrily slapping the water with his pan. "If they've got a brain amongst 'em, they'll ride for the flatlands. Cavalry's looking for 'em east, and the Shoshonis ride out west. Sioux scalp anybody they can find up north, or so I've heard. No, the mountains are no safe refuge for Shadrack Ashley, and it's mighty hard to disguise a one-armed man."

"You could be right," Seth said, dropping his chin. "It's hard to stand around, though. I was taught to fight back."

"So was Vance. He's dead."

Seth nodded sadly, then splashed his way back to his horse and led the animal toward what remained of the camp downstream. Willie resumed his labors.

He worked all morning, occasionally adding a few flakes to the pouch tied to his belt. Tildy brought him a couple of biscuits and some bacon around noon.

"Thanks," he told her as he sprawled out on the bank.

"What're you doin', Wil?" she asked. "You should be out there trackin' Shad Ashley."

"I've got no thirst for vengeance," he explained. "No hunger for killing anybody."

"I have!" she exclaimed. "I'd kill the whole bunch."

He frowned and ate his lunch. Then he stepped back into the shallows and began sifting sand again.

Seth returned a couple of hours later. The boy dipped a line in the creek and whistled a tune. The melody, "Sweet Betsy from Pike," had been one of Vance's particular favorites.

"He taught it to me," Seth explained. "I don't have the voice for ballads really. Janie Moffat did."

"Yeah, she was the singer," Willie remarked.

"Alex can play a mouth organ fair. Maybe if he's feelin' better tomorrow, he can come down and show you."

"Maybe."

"Ma said if I catch enough trout, she'll fry 'em up for everybody. You think you could eat one? If you'd come, Miss Tildy would, too. Ma says it's only fittin' for the bereaved to have a day off from cookin'."

"And your ma?" Willie asked. "Has she had a day off?"

"Althea took on the cookin', but I guess Ma's had her share o' labors, what with mindin' the little ones and all."

"Well, let me get rid of this pan, and I'll grab a pole. Maybe between us we can manage. I'd expect we could build up a fire, maybe even fry up some griddle cakes to go with the fish."

"You can cook?" Seth asked in surprise.

"Man has to learn to tend his own needs, Seth. No women along when you take to the trail, you know."

"Never thought o' that," Seth confessed.

"Well, you can't talk fish out of a pond. Let's see if some bait and a bit of patience won't do it."

Willie set aside his pan, cut a willow branch, and attached a bit of string. Seth provided the hook, and a bit of bacon left from lunch was offered as bait. Soon the first trout was plucked from the stream.

By suppertime, a dozen fish had been caught, cleaned, and filleted. Clark and Jake Moffat built a fire, and Althea Hagen molded griddle cakes from some cornmeal that had escaped the fire. Gump brought Tildy down, and the little company, most still wearing their mourning faces, enjoyed the supper. Afterward they sang camp songs. Alex even sat up and played a melody on his mouth organ.

The music bolstered Willie's spirits some, but it didn't drive away the phantoms lurking in the surrounding hills. There was no fire to mark Shad Ashley's camp, but everyone felt the outlaw's nearness. Later, when the others headed back to their camp and the fire had been doused, Willie walked alone beside the creek and stared at the distant stars.

"Lord, you take so much of the best," he whispered. "Why? Vance never did anyone harm. And that little Janie!"

The wind whispered a mournful tune through the cottonwoods on the far bank, and Willie took it for an answer. Even the wind grieved. Still, it seemed all too likely that death would strike again.

Back to the cabin, he found Tildy busy filling provision bags. Gump had finished cleaning and oiling the firearms. He was packing up his belongings.

"Going someplace?" Willie asked.

"After Ashley," Gump mumbled.

"And you?" Tildy asked, turning to Willie.

"I'm not," he told her.

"You can't let that old man go all alone!" she argued. "His eyes are no good in the dark now, and when the chill comes on, his fingers can hardly load a rifle."

"Good arguments for staying," Willie pointed out.

"Maybe I should go with him," she countered. "I'm not afraid."

"Fear's got nothing to do with it."

"Perhaps young Seth would make a better companion. He shows no reluctance."

"He doesn't know," Willie growled.

Tildy threw down the bag and raced out the door. Willie could hear her sobbing. He started to pursue her, but Gump blocked his path.

"It's time she did some cryin'," the old-timer declared. "Let her tend herself for a time. We need to talk."

"About what?"

"About Shad Ashley," Gump said angrily. "Trail's bound to grow cold soon. Wil, I know you're not afraid of him. You shot him twice. This has got to be done, and you know it."

"Gump, you know what this'll be like."

"Like that night we went after those Murphy boys? Sure, I know. I'm like as not to get myself killed, especially if I'm alone. That what you mean? Well, I've faced long odds before, Wil, and I've lived through tough times."

"Ashley is no man to give you a fair chance, Gump!"

"Nor you, either, for that matter. Wil, there's no other way for me. My road's got no turns left in it, son. It's straight as an arrow now the end's near. I leave at daybreak. Come with me."

"My heart's not in it."

"I buried my heart with young Vance," Gump explained. "That boy loved you like a brother. You had strong feelings for him as well. Look at Tildy! She's torn herself in two over this. I know you can't stand to see her in pain any more'n I can."

"I've buried friends before," Willie said, frowning.

"Boys?"

"Lots of 'em."

"You can lie to yourself, Wil Devlin, but you can't fool me. Your heart's as heavy as mine just now. Only thing to make any of us whole again is seein' Shad Ashley dangle from a cottonwood limb."

"I haven't been whole in fifteen years, Gump. One more killing won't patch my wounds. It'd only add to the darkness."

"I know what you feel, son. There's need of you, though."

"Need of me? For what, Gump? You'd think I was the angel of death sent to wreak vengeance on the wicked. I just want to be left alone to live in peace."

"It won't happen, Wil. I need you."

Willie dropped his chin onto his chest, then made his way out the door and back to the creek. As he walked, he stared overhead as the silvery moon darted in and out of a single stubborn cloud. The rest of the heavens were alive with stars.

"Wil?" Tildy called to him.

He stumbled to her side, and she rested her head on his weary shoulder. For a few moments they stood there silently. Then Willie swallowed deeply and gazed overhead.

"There were no stars in the sky the night before we hit the Yanks at Shiloh," he whispered. "I'd just turned sixteen, and I was so proud of the corporal's stripes on my sleeve. Then came the battle. Tildy, there's never been any brightness since that night."

"So, are you readyin' yourself for battle again?"

"You mean am I going?"

"You are, aren't you?"

"Guess I have to. Somebody's got to keep ol' Gump from riding into an ambush."

"You'll catch 'em, Wil. I know you will."

"Or else they'll kill us. That's how it is in a war."

At least the pain would end then, he thought. I almost welcome it.

She gripped his hand, and for a moment a warmth flowed through the both of them. Then the wind whined down from the north, sending a biting chill through Willie's back. It was the first bitter taste of what was sure to follow.

CHAPTER 9

In the predawn darkness, Willie shook himself awake and prepared for the difficult day that lay ahead. Tildy already had breakfast cooking, and Gump Barlow was outside readying the horses.

"We've got company," Tildy said as Willie dressed. "Look outside."

Willie peered through the door and saw the Hagens and Moffats crowded together on the hillside. Young Seth sat atop his horse, cradling a rifle and eager to take to the trail. John Moffat and his eldest boy, Clark, also appeared ready. Willie frowned and set off to argue against it.

"We've got a right to go," John Moffat argued. "I've suffered loss at least as grave as you have. I don't know this country like Gump, and I don't have your way with firearms, Devlin, but I imagine I can be of use just the same."

"Me, too," Seth declared.

"You don't recall anything I said to you yesterday, do you?" Willie asked. "Well, Erma," he added, turning to the boy's mother, "are you prepared to bury another so soon after Ethan?"

"He's got a strong will, that boy," Erma said, frowning. "I'd keep him if I knew how."

"I know how," Willie said, pulling the youngster from

his horse. "Hear me now, Seth. You've got a family to look after. They need you."

"They won't be safe so long as Ashley's out there," Seth complained. The thirteen-year-old set his jaw and faced Willie with an unflinching resolve.

"Walk with me a minute," Willie said, softening some. "Seth?"

The young man followed Willie to the creek.

"I'm not a boy anymore to hide when trouble's about," Seth argued. "I had bullets shot at me the other day. I could've been killed."

"And what's to say those raiders won't hit here again?" Willie asked. "Have you ever considered that? Somebody's got to stay behind and look after the women."

"Gump could stay."

"He knows these hills like his own nose, Seth. Do you? It's never easy staying behind, but . . ."

"Leave Clark here."

"You trust your ma to him? Tildy's a fair shot, but Alex is still on his back, and there's nobody else big enough to hold a gun steady, much less stand fast when trouble's coming. You know I'm right, son. As for Clark, I'll do my best to see he stays, too."

"You sure it's not 'cause you think I'm not up to the hunt?"

"I recall how you held your ground down at the creek," Willie said, placing a heavy hand on Seth's shoulder. "You stay here and guard the cabin."

"Cabin?" Seth asked.

"Yes," Willie said, leading the way back to the others. He soon explained what he meant.

"While we're gone, why don't you folks share the cabin?" he asked the others. "There's more than enough room, and it'll do young Alex good to be off the ground. Better protection against trouble, too."

"I never sent my family into another man's house," John Moffat protested. "We don't have a lot, it's true, but . . ."

"I don't say this because I think you can't provide for

your family," Willie said, shaking his head. "Look, Ashley may be where we expect, but he's done little we planned for so far. If he was to ride down here again, with us gone, I'd feel better knowing Tildy had some help."

"It's a good idea," Gump agreed.

"It is," Tildy said, wrapping an arm around little Jake Moffat. "This place wants the cackle of children just now. The walls are so silent I want to scream."

"Bein' in close quarters would be good for us all," Erma Hagen declared. "Share the chores, and we'd have each other for company."

"Moffat?" Willie asked.

"Agreed," Moffat said.

"Now, there's just one matter left," Willie said, waving Moffat off to the side. "That boy of yours is too young by half for what I have in mind."

"He's young all right," Moffat admitted. "But he's sound enough. He can shoot, and we'll need him, especially now you've talked Seth out of the ride."

"I'd talk you out of it, too, if I could," Willie responded. "This isn't going to be some Sunday march on a parade ground, you know. It'll be fighting close in, hard and deadly. Seems to me you've lost a young one already. Clark seems a mild boy, given to reading books and singing hymns. Fighting sours that sort of boy."

"So does buryin' a mother," Moffat added. "He goes."

Willie kicked a rock out across the hill and frowned. He didn't argue further, though, and after loading what supplies Tildy had packed in two flour sacks, he climbed atop his horse and motioned for Gump to lead the way eastward.

The four of them splashed across Rock Creek and continued into the pine-studded hills beyond. For a few minutes Gump had trouble locating traces of the outlaws in the rocky ground. Then he detected some bloodstained pine needles and waved his companions along.

The trail crossed a ridge and led some four miles up Big Atlantic Gulch, past abandoned mines and deserted camps northward, and away from Ft. Stambaugh. Bloodstains and bits of buffalo hair caught by pine branches or briars led them along. A dead horse lay astride a dusty trace that led west and east from the gulch.

"It's the old road to Atlantic City," Gump noted, gazing westward.

"Tracks all head east, Mr. Barlow," Clark pointed out.

"Hard to tell for certain," Gump answered. "I count three, maybe four horses goin' east. I thought there were more of 'em than that."

"One horse went down," Willie said, nodding at the fallen animal. "It's possible the others turned back or split off."

"That's what troubles me," Gump said, gazing uneasily behind him.

"Me, too," Willie confessed. "But we'd be smart to follow the best trail and tend this bunch. Later we can look for the others."

Gump searched the faces of his companions for a different opinion. None was offered, so the little company turned eastward on the sandy road.

"The old Gold Dollar's a couple of miles up this way," Gump explained. "Beyond that, Miner's Delight. There were some high times at that place while the gold lasted. I remember . . ."

Gump motioned for silence. Up ahead Willie thought he heard singing. He drew out his rifle and prepared to fire. Finally Gump waved them on, and the four riders cautiously continued.

They rode to within a quarter mile of the Gold Dollar. On the ridge overlooking the trail, collapsed adits attested to played-out mines. Willie kept a keen eye on each. A half-collapsed adit made a fine shelter for a sharpshooter.

"Hold up," Gump whispered as they finally spotted the ramshackle cabin that had once housed the Gold Dollar's miners.

"Oh, that place is finished," Moffat declared. "We were

up there ourselves before headin' on to Rock Creek. Nobody lives there anymore."

"Somebody does," Willie said, grimly pointing out the smoke rising from the chimney. A large man dressed in a buffalo cloak stood near the door. Willie ducked behind a stand of pines, and Gump bid the others do likewise.

"It's them," Moffat said. "Think they saw us?"

"Don't know," Gump answered. "Wil, care to scout it?"

Willie nodded, then dismounted. Gump climbed down as well. The Moffats remained to guard the horses.

As he wove his way through the rocks and pines, Willie felt oddly at home. How often he'd scaled ridges and scouted ahead of his company. He felt at ease in the shadows, in command. Gump noticed and left the ex-Confederate to lead the way.

Willie spotted the lookout first. Only a man used to reading the contours of the mountains would have noticed the pile of rocks that concealed the guard. Boulders cluttered the land, but most were on down the slope, not atop a ridge.

"See him?" Willie whispered. Now Gump had also detected the outlaw's vague shape. Both men slipped around below and behind the outpost and crept up for a closer look at the mine.

Only one of the buildings appeared to be occupied. From the noise inside, Willie judged two or three men to be there. Another busied himself tending the fire and preparing a pig for roasting.

"Four, maybe more," Gump announced when he and Willie rejoined the Moffats.

"Well, we're not badly outnumbered," Moffat declared. "If each one of us—"

"You taking charge?" Willie asked. Moffat scowled. "If not, listen well. We don't know if this is all of 'em, so it's best to wait for supper. They'll all be here for that."

"Would seem likely," Gump agreed.

"Soon as they're busy eating, we move in on 'em. I'll take the lookout myself. Moffat, you watch the road.

Gump, take the side door of the building. We all open up on the ones by the fire."

"They'll move back to the buildin'," Gump declared. "It'll be tough to root 'em out of there."

"We won't," Willie said, grinning. "Gump, you set the back of the place afire. That dry pine ought to go up straightaway. Then, if they don't surrender, we'll shoot 'em as they run from the flames."

"I say shoot 'em either way," Moffat argued.

"I'd rather see 'em hung," Gump objected. "Not much fun for 'em. Be a long time remembered, too, once the word gets around."

"We'll settle that later," Willie grumbled. "For now, everybody know what he's to do?"

"Not me," Clark said, staring nervously toward his father.

"You stay right here," Willie explained. "Guard the horses."

"What?" Clark protested. "I'm not afraid. I can use a rifle."

"Eager to be a hero, huh?" Willie asked. "Well, you've got the most important job, Clark. If those outlaws should slip past us, they only have one hope of escape. Our horses. They take 'em, we can't catch 'em afoot. And there's nothing to stop 'em hitting Rock Creek, either."

Clark continued to frown, but he nodded his obedience.

"Best have somethin' to eat and rest up," Gump suggested then. "Got a long wait ahead."

Gump proved right. For better than three hours the four of them sat in the pines, eating cold biscuits and dried venison while they fought to stave off a growing chill.

"Storm comin'," Gump observed. "Another night, maybe two."

"Your fingers tightening up?" Willie asked.

"Some," Gump confessed. "But I got two loaded pistols and a fifteen-shot Winchester. That ought to last me awhile."

"I'd say," Willie responded.

"Gump, you could take the far side of the road with Moffat if you wanted," Willie added when the others left to look after the horses. "I can handle the lookout and set the fire."

"Don't go changin' a good plan," Gump argued. "I'll hold up my end."

"Never dreamed you wouldn't," Willie told the old-timer. "Well, I guess it's time to head out now."

The old man nodded, then waved Moffat over.

"It's time," Willie said grimly. "Follow me. Remember to go in slow, keep out of sight. Pick 'em off one by one. Don't hurry your shots."

"I've been thinkin' about this plan," Moffat said sourly. "Seems to me you're takin' a lot on yourself. We've got a stake in it, too. Wouldn't we be better off chargin' 'em on horseback, blastin' the whole bunch in short order?"

"Depends," Gump answered. "There could be one holed up inside. And you might miss. Man on horseback, even at night, makes a fair target. Shoot from the cover o' pines, and you're close to invisible."

"But . . ."

"Look, Moffat," Willie said, fixing the miner with a heavy stare. "You want 'em dead, don't you? They will be. Trust me to know my business."

"I just hope you're right," Moffat said, turning to his son. Clark leaned against his father's side. The boy shifted his weight from one foot to the other, and he was clearly nervous.

"You all right, Clark?" Willie asked. "You know what to do?"

"He'll be fine when it comes down to it," Moffat insisted. "He's just seen his ma shot after all."

"I know what to do, all right, Mr. Devlin," Clark added. "I can handle horses. And if anyone gets past you, I'll shoot him."

Willie hoped not. It seemed the softness got worked out of boys far too early.

"It's a hard land, Willie," his father had told him long

ago. "To survive you have to be just as hard."

Willie was. But had he really survived?

He had other concerns, though. The moment to attack had arrived. Slowly, reluctantly, Willie cradled his rifle and headed onward. As he eased his way toward the lookout perch, he set aside his rifle, stripped off his coat, and crawled toward the rocks.

The lookout was too busy chewing a chunk of roast pork to notice the shadow creeping toward him. He hummed softly as he moved his hands over a small fire. Willie's left hand silenced the guard while the right hand brought a knife crashing down into the outlaw's chest.

Willie recalled how Ashley and the others had bruised and battered him, and the pain of cracked ribs and bashed skull blazed inside him. He heard their laughter, saw again Ashley's hated face.

Willie turned the knife, and a rush of air signaled the lookout's demise. Willie propped the villain up so that he seemed continually vigilant.

Gump handed the discarded rifle to Willie, stared coldly at the dead outlaw, and nodded toward the other raiders. By now they were enjoying their dinner and boasting of their exploits.

"We pretty well cleaned those folks out, didn't we?" one cried. "Did you see that boy at the creek with the rifle? They'll be sendin' babies up against us next."

"I hated we killed that woman in the rocker," another said. "The girl, too."

"We didn't know it was a woman," the first objected. "Besides, a skirt can shoot you just as dead as anyone else."

Willie blocked the voices out of his mind. He waited for Gump to reach the back of the building, then watched Moffat take cover behind the road. Then, slowly and silently, Willie raised his own rifle and aimed at the larger of the three outlaws gathered beside the fire. Willie counted. One. Two. Three. Then he fired.

The shot struck its target in the throat. The outlaw

gasped, jumped to his feet, and was sent flying by Willie's second shot. Moffat and Gump, meanwhile, opened up as well. The remaining outlaws made a mad rush toward the road. Neither arrived. Gump killed the closer with a clean shot through the head. Moffat hit the other in both legs.

By now the wretched old building was engulfed by flames. If anyone was inside, he went to his death silently, amid wicked flames and terrible heat. Willie examined the dead men, but each had both arms.

"Where's Ashley?" he screamed out. "Ashley? You out there?"

"Clark?" John Moffat called. "Clark, watch out for Ashley!"

Moffat then raced along to insure his son's safety. Willie stepped over beside the surviving outlaw.

"Where is he?" Willie demanded to know. "Well?"

"Who?" the dying raider asked, coughing violently.

"Shad Ashley. He brought you all to this. Tell me, where's he gone?"

"You Devlin?" the stricken man asked. Willie nodded. "Well, you hit us hard, I admit, but you missed ol' Shad. He and some of the other boys had some fun tonight. They said they had somethin' to finish over at Rock Creek."

"Something?" Willie asked, grabbing the outlaw by the collar. "What?"

"Had an appointment with a lady, I think," the villain said, laughing. "You think about that, will you?"

The fiend coughed again, then began narrating a tale of Ashley's favorite manner of torturing innocents. The outlaw then rolled over a bit, grabbed a hidden pistol, and turned it toward Willie. Before the pistol could emit its deadly projectile, though, Gump Barlow blasted the would-be assassin with a rifle.

Powder smoke shrouded the scene, and a startled Willie eyed Gump with gratitude.

"Guess I'm not too old to save your hide, eh?" Gump asked.

"I'd say not," Willie told the old man.

Clark and his father appeared then with the horses.

"That one," Willie explained, nudging the newly killed outlaw with the toe of his boot, "says Ashley doubled back on Rock Creek. I know we're tired, but I think we'd best ride like wildfire back there and help if we can."

"Shouldn't we bury these men?" Clark asked.

"Leave 'em for the buzzards," Gump suggested. "We've got other concerns."

Yes, Willie thought as he slid his rifle into its scabbard and pulled himself into the saddle. Tildy. The four of them set off southwest as one, with Gump leading the way. In all their minds were images of more death and heartache. It lent their horses wings with which to fly homeward.

CHAPTER 10

It proved a wild, furious ride through the dark, galloping first down the old trail toward South Pass City, then along the rocky bank of Big Atlantic Gulch, and finally across the hills to Rock Creek. Every screeching owl seemed to foretell of disaster and death. The whining wind tore at Willie's soul, exaggerated the terrifying scenes that tormented his thoughts.

A thousand nightmares haunted the four riders as they made their way across treacherous terrain on near-spent horses. Little Clark moaned and fought to hang on to his reins with exhausted fingers. John Moffat slowed his pace to stay closer to the boy. Gump gradually slowed as well. Only Willie charged on.

"You'll kill your horse," Gump warned when the others agreed to dismount and rest the animals a bit.

"Maybe," Willie admitted. "But it's others I fear'll be killed if I delay."

The words provided little comfort to the others, but they nevertheless rested their mounts. Willie stroked his own pony's nose and pleaded for another hour's effort. The horse snorted a reply, and Wille urged the animal onward.

He rode the final three miles to Rock Creek alone. Darkness clung to the hills like a heavy cloak, and it was impossible to see anything. Finally, as he grew closer to

Rock Creek, he detected a faint glow up ahead. Smaller pinpricks of light lit the scene here and there. A scent of singed cloth hung in the air.

I'm too late, Willie thought as he heard at last the surging waters of the creek. It's all over.

He eased his reins and let his weary horse saunter on toward the creek. Willie then dismounted, took a drink from the stream, and splashed across. The sound of shotgun hammers clicking into cock froze him.

"Who's there?" a voice called.

"Wil Devlin," he answered.

"Step over to the fire," a hoarse speaker commanded. "Now!"

Willie continued across the creek, then cautiously walked to the fire. On the opposite side, wielding a heavy shotgun in her hands, stood Althea Hagen. Nearby Seth held a rifle.

"You plan to shoot me?" Willie asked. "Well?"

"You were right," Seth explained. "Good thing we were all up at the cabin, else most'd likely be dead. They rode through like a cyclone."

"Tildy?" Willie asked, starting toward the smoldering cabin.

"She's tendin' the little ones," Althea explained. "They didn't hurt her."

"They didn't just ride down here to burn a cabin," Willie grumbled. "Tell me the whole thing."

"They caught us nappin'," Seth said, wiping his eyes. "I was down fetchin' water at the creek. They were all around us, just like last time. All of a sudden rifles opened up from everywhere. I hid behind a fallen cottonwood. Ma saw 'em. She grabbed a rifle and tried to give the little ones time to get to safety. I don't think she even got off one shot. Ashley killed her."

"He was too quick," Althea commented. "Ma, she wasn't a soldier."

Seth stumbled over, and Willie instinctively drew the boy close. Althea leaned on his other side, and for a moment he was comforting the youngsters. Then horses splashed into Rock Creek, and Seth broke loose, grabbed his rifle, and readied himself for another attack.

"Hold your fire," Willie warned. "Gump and the Moffats are coming."

Seth fired a warning shot, and Gump answered with a loud curse.

"You plan to do Ashley's work for him, boy?" the old-timer called as he led his horse across the creek. "Can't shoot at every noise, Seth!"

"It's what Ashley does," Althea complained.

"I look like that one-armed son of Satan?" Gump asked. Seth shook his head, and Gump grumbled about arming youngsters with rifles.

Willie escaped the quarrel and slipped up the hill toward the cabin. It was pretty well consumed by then. Cathleen Moffat huddled with the little ones under a few blankets. Alex Hagen, pale as death, feebly played his mouth organ.

"They shot us up somethin' awful," Jake Moffat explained. "I thought we would all die. Miz Tildy held 'em off, though."

"Sure did," Cathleen agreed. "Even at night, she found the mark with that rifle of hers."

Willie turned and searched for her. Tildy had apparently disappeared. As his eyes grew more accustomed to the darkness, though, he spotted her shadowy figure a dozen yards away.

"Tildy?" he called to her.

"I guess maybe you should've stayed after all," she mumbled. "You rode off one way, and Ashley hit us from the other. They killed Erma."

"So I heard," Willie said, wrapping his arm around her slender shoulders. "We got four of 'em at the old Gold Dollar Mine. Not the right ones, though."

"He's a devil, Wil!" she said angrily. "I didn't have a clue he was near till his men rode down on us. It's a miracle anybody's still breathin'."

"Well, even a devil needs men. We whittled him down to size."

"He had plenty of help here. Maybe half a dozen in all."

"Sometimes it seems there's no end to the no-accounts who'll throw in with the likes of Ashley. It was the same fighting the Murphy brothers. No sooner did we shoot a couple than four new men signed on."

"The trick's to shoot Ashley. There's just one of him."

"No, there are a thousand!" Willie barked. "Sure, they have different names and different faces, but they all share the same dark heart."

"Wil?"

"Don't you think I've got a right to sound a little bitter? All I ever asked for was a little peace. Now the war's come again, and there's no escaping what'll follow. First I want to get you back to your grandpa, though. Then I'll go after Shad Ashley if I have to do it alone."

"There's no place for me back at Grandpa's station. I'm not sixteen anymore, Wil. I won't pass the rest of my days fixin' breakfast for a bunch o' strangers at a stage stop. I buried my brother here, but that doesn't mean I've changed my mind about what I want."

"And that is?"

"A home. A man to share it with. Kids."

"There are plenty of those up on that hill."

"I think I'd rather grow my own," she said, grinning. "Well, Wil?"

"We'll see," he muttered. "First there's Ashley to take into account."

The killer was on Willie's mind much of the time. He and Gump dug a grave for Erma Hagen beside her slain husband, and young Seth collected the children. There was no Erma to read comforting words this time. John Moffat read verses from Erma's bloodstained prayer book. The children sat in stone-faced silence and stared at the smoldering ashes of the cabin.

"What's to come of us?" Seth asked afterward. "Now there's nobody to look after the little ones."

"You and Althea seem to be doing just fine," Willie observed.

"She's eleven, and I'm not full grown, Mr. Devlin. How can I earn a livin'? There's no work 'round here. We have no money, no family."

Willie nodded somberly.

"You're welcome to stay with us for now," Willie responded. "Tildy can use the help, and I don't mind company at the creek. Especially when I'm fishing."

"I'm afraid of this place," Seth confessed. "Every sound I hear puts me in mind of those raiders. Molly and Myrtle cry in their sleep, and Peter holds on to me all night."

"It's a heavy load life's handed you," Willie pointed out. "I'll bet you're up to the task, though. Who knows what's liable to happen? We might all strike a vein tomorrow."

"Or be dead," Seth muttered.

A bit later John Moffat spoke to Willie on the same subject. "I've known loss these last few days, too," Moffat said grimly. "I'll look after the Hagen kids. Shoot, Ethan and I were like brothers the past five years. I figure I owe him. Besides, Seth's a fair hand with the work, and Althea will be a big help to my Cathleen with the cookin' and cleanin'."

"You talked to Seth about it?" Willie asked.

"He said he'd already spoken to you," Moffat explained. "You know it's the best course for all. Tildy's wonderful with the little ones, but they need a father, too. I know your kind, Devlin. You aren't one to stay to see little Peter grown."

"No," Willie admitted. "It's best they go with you."

"I've never been one to ask another's help, but I've only got a couple of horses and a wagon left to my name. I was thinkin' maybe you could spare somethin' to help us get started."

"Money?" Willie asked. Moffat nodded, and Willie drew out the small roll of bills left from his days riding guard for George Wheaton's freight outfit. There was scarcely sixty dollars. "Not much to build a future with," Willie grumbled as he passed the money on to Moffat, "But it's yours."

"You'll keep somethin'?" Moffat asked.

"I got no need of it," Willie declared. "Not where I'm headed."

Willie turned away and stumbled to the creek. He dipped his hands in the chill stream, hoping to wash the dirt and blood from his hands. Traces of red clung to his fingernails, stained his clothes. No, it wasn't that easy to erase a nightmare!

"I hear Moffat's takin' in the Hagen brood," Gump said, sitting on a rock and gazing at the far ridge.

"Seems best," Willie declared.

"I thought maybe you'd take 'em in yourself. Tildy's grown fond of the girls, and . . ."

"I've no heart left for children," Willie declared. "Little ones would never make the trail I'm taking to."

"Ashley?"

"Ashley," Willie said sourly. "No matter where he's gotten to, I'll follow."

"You won't have a far ride," the old man said, pointing to a fire on the ridge above them.

"He's got to be crazy to stay so close."

"Does he?" Gump asked. "He can see every move we make. There aren't enough men or enough rifles to hold him off. Any of us leave, he's sure to strike."

"Kind of like going eyeball-to-eyeball with a rattler."

"True enough. All Shad's got to do is wait, bide his time till he decides the odds are in his favor. Meanwhile, we can't fetch help or supplies or anything else."

"Then I guess we'll rest a bit, then head up there tomorrow and settle matters."

"The numbers are in his favor, Wil," Gump argued. "If we turn toward South Pass City. . ."

"We? You mean Moffat and the kids, too? Lots of good places for an ambush on the trail to Willow Creek. Don't I know? My ribs still remind me of the last time I took that trail."

Gump dropped his head and muttered something. Willie raised his fist and shook it at the distant fire.

"Ashley, I'm down here waiting!" Willie cried. A chorus of laughter seemed to echo back. "Ashley, I'm not so easy to shoot as old women and little kids!" Willie added. "I put two bullets in your cursed hide. Next time I'll make certain the job's finished. Hear?"

The wind whined a lonely answer, and Willie scowled. Gump helped him up the hill, and they spread out their blankets at opposite ends of the sea of children tossing uneasily in saddle blankets and buckskin jackets.

Willie stared again at the distant campfire. "I'm here," the wind seemed to whine. "Come and see for yourself!"

Willie glared at it. He envisioned Ashley's jeering face arguing for a fresh attack.

Well, I'm here, too, Willie cried silently. Come and find your death, Shad. Let me end the weeping of this valley.

Willie lay back against the cold, hard ground and sought to find some rest. Moffat walked alongside, rifle in hand, standing watch. Later the others would take turns, too. For now, though, Willie allowed his heavy eyelids to close, shutting out the pain and suffering all around him. Sleep bore him elsewhere, and for a short time peace settled in.

CHAPTER 11

Willie sat atop the hill, looking down on his sleeping companions as the sun crept over the eastern horizon. He'd managed only an uneasy sleep. Now, staring at the flicker of yellow flame on the far ridge, his thoughts more than ever filled with Shadrack Ashley.

What's holding you here? Willie wondered. Why wait? Come down and finish with us!

Willie knew from the flaying arms of the children that they, too, feared another raid. Why not? Had peace ever come when war was so near?

As the others greeted the rising sun with moans and sleepy yawns, Tildy sent Clark Moffat and Seth Hagen off to gather firewood. Soon the boys had a fair fire blazing. Tildy then rolled the last of the flour into biscuit squares.

"Afraid breakfast will be a bit scant this mornin'," she announced. "We're out of flour now, and close to the bottom of the bean barrel as well."

"I wish they'd spared Betsy," Cathleen complained. At least with the cow there'd been milk. The poor creature had been driven well down the creek, then shot so that even her meat was spoiled by the time the carcass was located.

"There's always fish," Seth suggested. The other youngsters groaned.

"It's time we made a trip to Haybro's," Tildy declared. "For now, though, maybe somebody could shoot a deer or some rabbits. Wil?"

"Once the danger ebbs," Willie answered. "As things lie, I hate to leave you short a rifle."

"Mr. Moffat and Gump will be here," Seth pointed out. "Miz Tildy shoots just fine, too, and Cathleen's learnin'. I could go with you."

Willie frowned as fear flashed across the faces of the younger Hagen children. Althea clasped her older brother's hand, and little Peter nestled in beside Seth's feet.

"It can wait some," Willie said, grinning at Peter in particular. "Fish make for a fine lunch. Later, we'll see about hunting."

As the others relaxed, Willie stared again at the distant ridge. It was hunting of another kind altogether that was truly needed. Shad Ashley's carcass would be a far more welcome sight than a bull elk just then.

"Well, here's breakfast," Tildy called then, and all other thoughts were set aside. She meted out a square biscuit to each person, then carried the skillet to the creek for scrubbing. Willie noticed she kept nothing for herself. Moffat divided his square among his younger children. Gump split his between Molly and Myrtle Hagen. Willie turned his over to Seth.

"Was my cookin' that bad?" Tildy asked when Willie joined her at the creek.

"I didn't notice you taking a square," he responded.

"Well, I didn't ride over half the countryside yesterday either. You need to keep up your strength."

"One biscuit won't make much difference. I never eat much in the morning anyway."

"Wil, we've got to have some fresh meat for those children. They look half-starved. I never dreamed they were eating so poorly."

"It's always been the worst part of a gold camp," Willie muttered. "The kids. I've seen whole bunches left behind to forage for themselves. Those that survive run to men like Shad Ashley 'cause he promises 'em a fortune. Risk doesn't much shake 'em. They know death's shadow."

"Think you could get to town and back today?"

"A man alone won't get there at all," Willie told her. "If Ashley holds off through the afternoon, I'll see what I can find."

She gave him a warm smile and drew him close. As they sat together watching the bubbling creek, worries seemed miles away. Soon, though, the chattering children swept them back to the present.

"I was wonderin', Miz Tildy, if maybe we oughtn't to get everybody a bath?" Cathleen asked. "Me, I know I need to wash the smoke and grit out of my hair, and the little ones are as bad."

"It's a good notion," Tildy agreed. "Split the boys and girls. You take—"

"We already done it, ma'am," Seth broke in. "Cathleen and Althea took half Ma's cake of soap. They'll go downstream past our old camp. Clark and I'll get the boys down 'round the bend. Each is out o' sight o' the other that way."

"Fair enough," Willie observed. "Cathleen, maybe you'd better take my rifle with you, though. Trouble could still be nearby."

"I'll take mine," Tildy said, waving Willie away. "I need a good scrubbin' myself. You keep yours. Take it with you and get a wash yourself. Wil, you look to've escaped a coal mine."

The children laughed and pointed to the grimy stains on Willie's shirt and trousers.

"We'll wash the clothes, too," Althea said. "Even the boys' things. I'll stay back to fetch 'em."

"And what'll we wear in the meanwhile?" Seth asked.

"A blanket," Willie said, pointing to the bedding on the hillside. "Or in Peter's case, a kerchief."

The boy frowned, but Seth managed to elicit a grin by explaining how Indian boys wore scarcely more. Soon the children divided into their separate bands and headed for the creek. Tildy escorted the girls, and John Moffat looked after the boys. Willie followed Seth to where his brother Alex rested.

"Think you can stand a washing, Alex?" Willie asked.

The ten-year-old nodded, and Willie carefully picked up the boy. Alex seemed light as a feather pillow, and Willie, weary as he was, had no trouble carrying him to the creek. Seth helped Alex shed his clothes, and as the boys splashed into the shallows, even old Gump arrived.

"Couldn't let you young critters have all the fun," the old-timer explained as he jumped into the midst of them. "Pass that soap."

Willie stood guard until Moffat finished his bath. Then the two exchanged duties. Even so, Willie kept close to shore, near his rifle, and away from the cavorting bathers.

He was glad Tildy couldn't see them. In her worst dreams, she wouldn't have suspected how pale and thin those boys could appear. Grimy faces and filthy clothes could hide sunken cheeks and narrow waists. In truth, the figures bobbing in the creek were little more than frameworks of bone with skin stretched tightly on top.

It ate at Willie. He watched Seth and his companions chase one another through the shallows and recalled how Vance had run in like fashion the previous summer. A wave of sadness descended on the dark-browed veteran. Again he gazed up at the ridge. No campfire, not even a wisp of smoke, met his eyes. And yet Willie knew Ashley was up there.

For a time the laughter of the children chased away his gloom. Gump carried little Peter and Stuart Moffat around on his shoulders. Alex seemed to brighten for the first time since being laid low.

"Somethin' botherin' you, Mr. Devlin?" Seth asked, sitting beside Willie in the shallows. "Seem worried."

"Am some," Willie admitted. "But mostly I look at you and your brothers, and I remember another boy."

"Vance?"

Willie nodded, and Seth frowned.

"I liked Vance," Seth declared. "He was sort of a big

brother. Was him taught me to wind my string around my pole so I could let it out or take it in as I pleased. I miss him some. Not like Ma and Pa, but some."

"You've got a small army to look after now. I don't envy you much."

"It won't be any too easy, I suppose, but Clark's close to as old as me, and he'll help. Once Alex is back on his feet, he'll lend a hand, too. Truth is, I don't know I could stand it if they didn't need me. See, that keeps me from thinkin' too much."

Willie nodded. Maybe that was his trouble. He thought too much. Once he'd relied on instinct. Now he—well, he wasn't at all sure of anything, especially himself.

Once everyone had his bath, and the clothes were scrubbed and hung up to dry, Willie set the boys to fishing for their lunch. In an hour or so, a dozen fine trout were coaxed from the creek, cleaned, and set frying in skillets.

"That'll fill a few of those bellies," Tildy remarked. "I never saw children so thin, not even in the Shoshoni winter camps."

"I'll see if I can shoot some supper," Willie promised after devouring his share. "If I can't find a deer, I know where some ducks are passing the summer. They make fine eating."

"A deer would provide some needed clothing, though. Some of those woolens won't survive another washing."

Willie glanced over at the small figures still huddling in blankets. Yes, a journey to Haybro's was in order. But first he'd shoot some supper.

He set off alone down the creek a hundred yards or so, then climbed into the rocky hills beyond. He wished there were buffalo or elk to shoot, great creatures who would pass their strength to the frail children back at Rock Creek. A buffalo or elk hide would fend off the worst chills of winter, too. Willie found traces of neither. What he did spy set his hair on edge.

On the far side of the creek a pine branch moved. Then

another. Willie detected a flash of red flannel. Then a face appeared.

"Ashley," Willie muttered as he turned back toward his camp. Lord, give me a little time to get back, he prayed.

Shad Ashley seemed in no particular hurry to launch his attack, and Willie's feet carried him swiftly through the willows and cottonwoods along Rock Creek back to the others.

"What's wrong?" Tildy cried when he stumbled to her side.

"That!" Willie answered, pointing to the lead horseman now splashing up the creek.

"Not again," John Moffat cried. "Children, get down!"

"Not here," Willie said, passing his rifle to Seth and taking Alex in his arms. "In those rocks down at the creek. Hurry! There's no time to waste."

Gump and Moffat swung their rifles to bear on the raiders while Willie shepherded the youngsters to their refuge. A wall of boulders lined the creek on one side, but there was little cover from the creek itself. Willie hoped to build a barricade of sorts to shield them, but the raiders provided no chance. They fired their rifles wildly and thundered toward the rocks.

Willie was settling Alex behind a boulder when the first bullet sliced a nearby rock. Seth handed over the rifle as a volley battered the boulders. Willie took aim and sent the lead horseman to an early grave.

Gump and Moffat stumbled along moments later, and Tildy opened fire as well. The raiders appeared confused. Their targets had seemingly disappeared. Ashley kept out of range, though, and once he spotted the weakness of the position, waved his five surviving companions back across the creek.

"Listen carefully," Willie instructed the children. "They'll come from the creek this time. I want you to keep low. If you can, keep behind these rocks."

Cathleen shielded little Stuart and her sister June, and Althea half buried Peter in a hollow spot. Willie gave his small charges an encouraging grin, then set about the grim job of keeping Ashley's raiders at bay.

There was no charge this time. Instead the outlaws kept to the trees and brought a murderous fire to bear.

Willie bit his lip and swallowed a growing bitterness. What chance was there in such a fight? As bullets crashed through the limbs of the surrounding cottonwoods, as they sent splinters of rock showering down on the children, Willie fired back at the powder flashes.

"Keep low," Gump said as the howling children began to panic. "They're still way over on the far side of the creek."

"Ma died right over there," Molly Hagen lamented. "Seth?"

"You're all right, Moll," Seth assured the weeping girl.

"That's right," Gump echoed. "Wil, you got some cartridges to spare in that belt of yours? I loaded the last of mine in my magazine last night."

"I'm low, too," Tildy called.

Willie glanced down at his pistol belt. There were but two shells left, and they fit his pistol.

"Tildy, there was a box of shells in my saddlebags," he explained. "You pull them out?"

"We shot 'em up last night," Seth grumbled. "Only way we could keep 'em off was to keep shootin'."

"Not your fault," Willie grumbled. "Best save our ammunition for later, though. Don't shoot unless you've got a clear target."

It was a recipe for disaster. With no return fire to discourage them, Ashley's raiders closed the distance. Their aim improved. Willie watched in dismay as volleys of rifle fire crept gradually closer.

"Seems a poor conclusion to an eventful life," Tildy told him as she settled in at his side. "I'm out of bullets."

"Take this pistol and wait for their charge," he explained. He also gave her the two spare bullets left on his belt.

"Where are you goin'?" she asked.

"Where I can do some good," he explained. He then crawled past the cowering children, on past the boulders, and along the line of cottonwoods that flanked the attackers.

"They're done for!" Ashley shouted then. "Let's go, boys!"

Two raiders started toward the creek, and Willie sent a bullet crashing into the first one's chest. The second dove to the ground, narrowly escaping a like fate.

"Somebody's gotten into those trees, Shad!" a voice called.

Ashley rode out on his horse and prepared to drive Willie into the open. At that moment, though, a bugle call split the afternoon air. Tom Reed waved his arm in the air, and a dozen bluecoats roared down the creek. On their flanks came Raventail and a like number of Shoshoni scouts. The howling Indians sent the raiders in flight. Bullets sought them out and sent each of the outlaws spinning and falling along Rock Creek.

Willie hardly realized what had happened. In an instant it was over. The soldiers simply swept the creek clean of raiders, and the Shoshonis chased down the sole straggler and carved the life from him.

"It's all right, folks," Lieutenant Reed called. "You're safe now."

The children raised a cheer, and Tildy rushed out to thank the cavalrymen. Willie moved more cautiously. He walked past the corpses, turning them over so that their lifeless eyes gazed skyward. There were five at the creek and the one he'd killed earlier up the hill. Shad Ashley was not among them.

"These are the ones who killed my people," Raventail said as his warriors dragged the corpses off into the trees. "They will never kill again."

"Did you see the leader?" Willie asked. "The one-armed man."

"He fled," Lieutenant Reed explained. "I sent a squad

after him. Don't worry. We'll hound him to hell if it's needed."

"It will be," Willie assured the lieutenant.

"Meanwhile, I'll see the supply wagons are brought up. These folks look in need of a meal."

"Thanks," Willie said. "And if you have any blankets to spare . . ."

"We don't," Lieutenant Reed said, "but I'm certain we can find some things in the knapsacks of those raiders. There were blanket rolls, too, I believe. I'm sure those men would want these little ones to have them."

"Sure they would," Willie muttered.

"I thought we'd waged our last campaign together when we finished the Murphys," the lieutenant declared. "You just don't seem to be able to steer clear of trouble, do you, Mr. Devlin?"

"Guess not," Willie confessed. "I'm glad you seem able to track it down, though. You saved my hide this time, Lieutenant."

"Well, you're welcome to save mine next," the soldier said grinning.

CHAPTER 12

Lt. Tom Reed did more than set Raventail's Shoshonis and a squad of cavalry on Shad Ashley's trail. The lieutenant helped John Moffat load his family into a supply wagon. The Hagen children climbed aboard a second wagon.

Wil Devlin looked on sadly as a half-dozen soldiers escorted Moffat and the youngsters to Ft. Stambaugh. From Seth Hagen came a sad, solemn wave. The boy looked older than Willie could ever remember.

By noon Rock Creek seemed nearly deserted. Except for the scars left by cabin ashes and the row of crosses marking graves, the creek differed little from most of the ghostly streams and abandoned settlements in the South Pass area.

"Maybe it's time we were leaving, too," Willie whispered to Tildy.

"Not just yet," she insisted. "I don't have the heart for starting over. And we have no supplies, remember?"

Willie started to suggest a trip to Haybro's, but he swallowed the words when he saw Tildy's eyes turn to the lonely ridge where Vance rested. Grief left fresh wounds. They would need time to heal.

The absence of the children cast a haunting silence across the valley. Tildy was left with little to do, and Willie found himself missing Seth's company down at the creek. Fishing wasn't the same. Nothing was.

In the days that followed, summer smiled on the land. Blankets of wildflowers splashed shades of blue and yellow and red across hills too long brown and barren. New life bounded along the creek. Fawns darted through the thickets, and curious ground squirrels visited the camp each morning.

The creek continued to provide plenty of trout, but Willie took little interest in fishing. He often sat on a boulder and dipped his line in the water, recalling better times when he'd fished the Brazos with his brother Jamie or the Cobb youngsters. As he pulled a trout from the chill water, he listened to the lonely call of the wind whining through the willows and cottonwoods.

"Where have you brought me, wind?" he asked.

It wasn't the wind's way to answer, and the ears that once might have understood had been deafened by pain and hardship.

Three days after the others left, old Gump declared it was time to resume their labors. Willie followed the old-timer to Rock Creek, and they worked the streambed from dawn to midday. Tildy remained on the bank.

"It was this gold foolishness that brought us here," she grumbled. "It cost Vance his life."

Gump argued the point. Willie left her to the sadness he, too, felt. It seemed to grow in the silence of the afternoon, threatening to strangle him. When he could stand it no longer, he took his rifle into the hills in search of game.

"It's time we admitted there's no more color to be had in this creek!" Gump announced when Willie returned with a pair of rabbits. "It's time we looked elsewhere."

"Where?" Tildy asked, planting a hand on each hip.

"Oh, sometimes you can scrounge a bit of gold out of others' leavin's," Gump explained. "We can start with the rock 'round the stamp mills. I've seen as much as twenty ounces dug from some. Later we can sift through the slag heaps. Then . . ."

"We become scavengers?" Willie asked. "I've seen 'em lots of times, ragged folks hanging on in ghost towns, hoping somebody might have missed a vein after all. It's a fine way to starve. And if you get desperate enough—well, there's always Ashley's road."

"No!" Tildy shouted.

"Then what?" Willie asked. "You can't farm this country. It's all rock. There's no livestock, and plenty of Indians! Tildy, I know what's in your heart. Mine's heavy as well. But it's time we left."

"We need things," she said, sniffling as she gazed at the distant hills. "Coffee, flour, vegetables if they can be had. I'd love a can of peaches. Someone's got to go to Haybro's."

"Someone?" Willie asked.

"You," she answered.

"Gump knows this country better than me," Willie argued. "It's not been so long since Ashley rode through here, and—"

"If there's trouble on the road, you'll be better at handlin' it than me," Gump declared. "As for 'round here, I've still got a decent eye with a rifle."

"We could all go," Willie suggested.

"No, it's a job for one," Tildy said, lightly touching Willie's hand. "I'll make up a list. You can pack the goods back on the extra horse."

Willie grasped her hand and nodded.

Early the following morning he set off toward South Pass City. Unlike his earlier journey, this time Willie kept his eyes ever alert for signs of danger on the trail. Ashley was likely dangling from a cottonwood branch by now, but the hills between Rock Creek and South Pass were inhabited by knots of scavengers who would descend on a lone rider carrying gold if given half a chance.

Willie gave them none. Whenever he passed even a shadow of a camp or smelled the smoke of a dead campfire, he made certain the long barrel of his Winchester could be seen resting across his knee. It discouraged interest.

The journey itself wasn't so long or difficult that a rider couldn't return in a single day. Willie planned to do just that. He reasoned whatever danger there really was, it was greater while sleeping, especially in the wild, largely lawless hotel in South Pass City.

The town had seen its heyday, though. When Willie arrived, he found the long main street that ran parallel to Willow Creek largely deserted. A couple of cows grazed near the old schoolhouse, but there were no children inside to complain. Many of the remaining dwellings were boarded up. Where once music had drifted out the double doors of one saloon or another, now only ghostly silence met his ears.

Willie spotted Jonas Haybro unloading a supply wagon. Or so it seemed. Only upon closer examination did Willie realize the man was piling supplies into the back of the wagon, not off-loading goods as would have been expected.

"Well, it's Devlin!" Haybro called, setting aside his work long enough to greet the oncoming rider. "I'd thought you clear o' this country weeks past. Still ridin' with the Bonner kids and old Gump?"

"With Tildy anyway," Willie said, sadly climbing off his horse. "We had the misfortune to be visited by Shad Ashley. Vance's dead."

"Oh, no," Haybro lamented. "Pop'll take that news hard, especially as Ashley burned the station not long past. And Gump?"

"Cantankerous as ever. Rock Creek's played out, though. I came to trade with you for some goods. We thought to get a fresh start elsewhere."

"There's talk of gold in Montana," Haybro said as Willie passed over the gold pouches. "Got to skirt the Sioux to get there, though."

"Tildy's kind of sour on mining," Willie explained. "I

thought we might go back to Cheyenne, maybe find her a little rooming house, or a small inn."

"Towns spring up down along the Union Pacific. We're headed that way ourselves. I've got a brother who's got a place halfway built already at Green River Station. They could likely use an inn there, too."

"I'll tell Tildy," Willie promised. "First I'd best get the supplies."

"Sure," Haybro agreed as Willie secured his horses to a hitching rack. Then they entered the store together.

Willie hardly recognized the place. Most of the shelves were already bare, and dust coated a few.

"You've known some lean times of late, too, I guess," Willie observed.

"Oh, it's the way with goldfields, Wil. You know some days when you make a fortune in a few hours. Most of the time it ebbs and flows for a few years before dyin' out. I've put my share o' coin away. The wife misses civilization, too. She's gone on ahead with the lead wagon, but she left some spiced beef and cold biscuits. Hungry?"

"Now that you mention it," Willie confessed. Haybro waved the way to a deserted table, then brought out the food. It was far from a feast, but it exceeded what Willie would have managed on his own.

"I recall stoppin' at Bonner's station on my way to South Pass," Haybro said, stretching his arms out. "That night Tildy cooked up chicken 'n' dumplin's, and I thought I'd never taste the like again. Was careful to keep my thoughts to myself, though. The wife isn't the best cook, but she isn't terribly tolerant of me sayin' the same."

"Yvette sure knows her way around a stove, though," Willie said, remembering how Haybro's daughter had prepared dinner when Willie and his freight crew had visited South Pass City.

"She was at that. Course she got herself married off last winter, Wil. Place started to seem empty the day she left. Just got worse since. Now it's time to close up and move on."

Willie knew the feeling. And as he checked items off Tildy's list, he fought off the flood of recollections assaulting his mind. He shook away the faces of friends who'd ridden into South Pass City with Wil Devlin the first time. He tried not to dwell on what had clearly passed into memory. It wasn't completely possible, though.

Haybro felt it, too. As they loaded the supplies onto the packhorse, the storekeeper narrated a tale of the boom days at Willow Creek and the big strikes made in the hills beyond. Finally, after Willie tied the last sack of flour to the back of the packhorse, Haybro produced a bottle of yellowish liquid and poured two small glasses.

"This stuff got a label?" Willie asked.

"Too good to have one," Haybro declared. "Green River corn, the kind that burns your throat and reminds you you're alive."

"So, what do we drink to?" Willie asked.

"To old times," Haybro suggested.

"To better times," Willie responded.

"Agreed," Haybro said, touching his glass to Willie's. The two men sipped the whiskey slowly. It fought off a chill Willie had felt creeping into his gut, and if it burned a man's throat—well, it also revived his soul.

"Guess my luck's improving," Willie said as Haybro waved a couple of slender-shouldered boys toward the goods remaining inside the store. "I might've missed you altogether in another day or so."

"You would have," Haybro assured him. "We'll be out of here by nightfall."

"Leaving a dead town behind," Willie muttered.

"Town's been dead awhile. Look at the place. Only ones left are those with no other place to go. Scavengers and orphans."

Willie stared at a trio of children skulking behind the old livery. One of them could have been a twin to Seth Hagen. It was what happened all too often. Parents died, or fled, leaving the youngsters to fend for themselves.

"I've rounded up half a dozen to help me move out,"

Haybro explained. "They're fair workers, and I think the wife's taken 'em to heart. We'll likely bring 'em along to Green River."

"And the others?"

"Will find their way," Haybro said sadly as he refilled the glasses. "Some will sign on with the stage line. Some of the older boys can join the cavalry. The really little ones will die off or get taken in by some rancher or traveler. And a few will get hold of a gun and make their livin' that way. It's nothin' new to you, though, is it?"

"No," Willie admitted. "Doesn't warm me much to say so."

"Nor me," Haybro said, emptying his glass.

"To better times," Willie called again as he sipped the whiskey. "Best of luck to you, Jonas."

"And to you, Wil Devlin," Haybro said, taking the glasses and flinging them against the wall of the store. "Give Tildy my best, and pass along my regards to that old mule Gump."

"I'll do that," Willie promised.

Willie tied the reins of the packhorse to the back of his own saddle, then mounted up. As he turned eastward and started back toward Rock Creek, he passed a pair of urchins staring up with half-starved eyes.

"There's no milk and honey where I'm riding," he called to them. "Better you find your own way."

The children only stared glumly. They had learned better than to expect anything different.

"Come on, boy," Willie urged his horse as they crossed the grassy hillside behind the livery and headed for Willow Creek. "We've got fresh flour. I'll bet Tildy cooks us up some biscuits. Maybe she'll make a cobbler with that can of peaches."

The horse seemed to respond to Willie's words. It stepped faster, and the heavily laded pack animal had to strain to keep pace. Soon they left the town behind and climbed into the hills beyond.

Willie rode back to Rock Creek with a heavy heart. It

was as if another chapter of his life was drawing to an end, and though it had not been a time full of warmth and affection, riding on into the unknown again filled Wil Devlin with fresh dread. Gloom etched fresh wrinkles in his forehead, and if not for the recent memory of Ashley's ambush, Willie might have let his mind wander in search of the better times he and Haybro had toasted.

There was also the task of keeping the packhorse on the trail. The animal was unaccustomed to its heavy load and often sought to escape by dislodging the supplies. If not brushing against the limbs of spruce and pine trees, the horse would shake or buck. The pack remained in place, though. Willie was no novice at securing supplies.

He was still a half-mile away when he smelled the pork roasting on a distant fire. Gump had spoken of hunting one of the wild pigs descended from more domestic porkers once raised near Miner's Delight, and Willie decided the old-timer must have aimed true. The flour would be particularly welcome, as would the sack of potatoes and carrots he'd convinced Haybro to part with.

When Willie topped the ridge and descended toward the creek, Tildy met him with a smile. Her eyes remained clouded with pain and grief, but she was unmistakably cheered by his return.

"I've got a pig on the spit," she said, bounding along as he approached. "Did you manage everything?"

"Did just fine," Willie told her. "Haybro was in a mood to sell. He's headed south, going into business with his brother at Green River Station. South Pass City's a ghost town."

"So is this place," she added as Willie dismounted. While he unsaddled his weary horse, Tildy inspected the supplies. She was especially pleased to see the vegetables, but the peaches brought another smile.

"Everything you need, eh?" Willie asked.

"Maybe we should have a cobbler," she countered. "Kind of a farewell feast, so to speak."

"Then you're agreeable to leaving?" he asked.

"Gump's been after me all day about it," she explained. "It's hard leavin' Vance up there all alone."

"He's not alone, Tildy. He's got the sun in the day and the stars at night. He has the mountains, the deer, the birds. And we'll remember him no matter where we are."

"I know," she agreed. "The flowers up there are so pretty. He loved bright colors, though he was shy about sayin' so. It bothered him some to be so small. He thought he had to put on a hard face so folks wouldn't think him still a boy."

"Yes," Willie said, shuddering. "Hurried himself into a man. And into a grave."

Gump appeared then, and they shook off their gloom. The old-timer entertained Willie with the tale of hunting the wild pig while Tildy busied herself preparing the food. As the pork sizzled, the potatoes browned, and the cobbler bubbled in a Dutch oven, Tildy spoke of leaving.

"It's time," Gump agreed straight off. "Little point to hangin' 'round now. No gold to pan, and there's bitter memories hereabouts. Best we be out of their shadow."

"Yes," Tildy whispered.

Willie frowned. He knew it wasn't that simple. Shadows had a way of stretching across whole mountainsides, and memories followed a man.

"We best pack up and head out tomorrow," Gump concluded. "Got fresh meat for the trail, lots of supplies, and . . . Wil, you did think to get shells for the rifles?"

"And the pistols," Willie answered. Strange how high a price a potato can bring up here, he thought. There's never a short supply of bullets, though. Death came cheap in these mountains.

Tildy helped Gump take the pork off the fire then, and soon Willie gazed down at a plate of roast pork and fried potatoes. He cast aside his other thoughts and ate.

CHAPTER 13

Willie often thought he was good at leaving places. He wasn't. Memories, as always, hovered in the shadows, and he knew they couldn't be left behind as easily as the bubbling waters of Rock Creek or the pine-studded mountains.

Tildy's face betrayed like feelings. While Willie and Gump readied the saddle horses and tied supplies on the back of the packhorse, she placed flowers beside the simple wooden crosses above the creek. She'd vanished earlier, and Willie knew she'd been up on the ridge to pass a few final moments with Vance.

When she returned, Gump helped her into the saddle.

"It's time we made a fresh start," she announced as her companions mounted. "Where to?"

"Haybro says there are lots of places down south that need inns and such," Willie told her. "The railroad's begun to draw crowds in its coaches. Not everybody cares for California, either."

"I hear there's been a fresh strike up in Montana," Gump said, gazing northward. "We'd be in on the front of it. That's where the fortune's to be made."

"I don't need a fortune," Tildy replied. "Just some peace."

Willie nodded his agreement, and Gump led the way eastward. As they rode, Willie gazed back at the deserted camp. They'd left little behind to mark their passing. Soon wind and rain would erase even that. Grass would cover the charred ashes of their campfires, and what remained of the cabin would rot away and vanish by first snow.

"No one would ever know we'd been there," Tildy mumbled as she passed Willie and took station behind the packhorse. "That seems strange. I have so many memories of the place."

"We've left reminders," Willie said, nodding toward the row of crosses, then staring up the slope where Vance lay.

"Yes," she whispered sadly. "We left behind the best of us."

Willie thought once more of the violent morning that had torn his world apart again. But in the end, it was Vance's laughter, his foolish pranks, and his youthful courage that Willie recalled. As Gump snaked his way through the hills, Willie tried to concentrate on the trail ahead. But the past was too much with him, and the memories continued to haunt his thoughts.

By midday Gump had led them close to fifteen miles beyond Rock Creek. Ft. Stambaugh and the abandoned mines at Miner's Delight were well behind them now. Ahead the Sweetwater River gathered runoff from the slopes of the Antelope Hills as it surged eastward toward its eventual junction with the North Platte.

"Where are you takin' us, Gump?" Tildy finally called.

"To familiar ground," he announced. "The Sweetwater Flats."

"I've been there," she reminded him. "Comin' west, remember?"

"On the old Oregon Trail," Gump said, pausing long enough to flash a grin at her. "There are stage stations set up all along the Sweetwater, and I figure we can find work there easy enough."

"Maybe," Willie grumbled. "There's work down south, too."

"Railroad town's no place to live," the old man argued.

"Used to be good game out this way. Antelope in summer. Buffs, too."

"Seems to me the Cheyenne and Sioux hunt this country," Willie said, anxiously eyeing the strange terrain.

"You'll not let a few Indians discourage you now, will you, Wil? Besides, I've never been bothered by Sioux."

"I have," Willie countered.

In the end, it wasn't Sioux they encountered, though. Down where a nameless creek emptied into the river, three tall lodges and a neat row of Sibley tents marked an army encampment. Moments after observing the camp, Willie spotted Raventail and three companions approaching.

"Hello," Willie said, offering the Indian his hand. "Didn't expect any company out this way."

"Nor I," Raventail declared. "Come, join our camp. The lieutenant is eager to speak to you."

"Lieutenant Reed?" Willie asked.

"Yes," Raventail answered gravely.

Willie exchanged a worried glance with Gump. Neither the Shoshonis, nor the cavalry, either, appeared pleased with their visitors.

Lieutenant Reed had always been both helpful and sympathetic. Now another side of the officer presented itself. The lieutenant met his guests stiffly, and angry words followed.

"You crazy, Devlin?" Lieutenant Reed shouted. "Bringing a woman through this country? The three of you alone with a packhorse straining under its load! You're inviting trouble."

"What manner of trouble?" Gump asked. "We can tend ourselves, you know."

"I know nothing of the kind," the lieutenant responded. "I buried three trappers yesterday who thought they were safe up here. The Sioux are none too hospitable. Always before they've kept to the north side of the Sweetwater, but lately some of 'em have the itch to stir up trouble. And you'd ride right into the heart of their country packing goods and carrying repeating rifles?"

"Lieutenant," Tildy complained, "I first traveled the Sweetwater when I was ten years old."

"Well, you're not ten now!" the lieutenant reminded her. "And you've not been through here of late. I don't take you for a fool, Miss Bonner. Please don't think me one."

"I don't," Tildy said, sighing. "It's just that—"

"No point to this," Gump interrupted. "Nobody's about to change his mind. We'll stay the night with you, Lieutenant, and afterward we'll stay clear o' Sioux or anybody else you worry over."

Willie realized the soldiers suspected Gump would do no such thing, but they all knew arguing would accomplish nothing. Gump began unsaddling the animals. Willie set off to visit Raventail.

"So, you've seen Sioux hereabouts, have you?" Willie began.

Raventail nodded grimly, then sketched a map of the Sweetwater in the dirt. The Shoshoni then pointed out a Sioux encampment ten miles downstream.

"Stayed on as a scout, eh?" Willie then asked. "I figured after you settled with Ashley, you'd probably head on home."

"As I will," Raventail replied.

"You didn't chase him down?"

"He is clever, that one," Raventail said, grinding his toe into the earth. "And these bluecoats make too much noise. We chased him out of the hills, but the Sioux kept us from going on. I hope they wear his scalp now."

"They will if they find him," Willie said, spitting the bitter taste from his mouth. "This comes as hard news. He's a snake all right. He'll hole up in some spot till the soldiers tire of looking for him. Then he'll collect some more men, and it'll be just like before."

"My eyes are on him. He won't escape," Raventail vowed.

He has already, Willie thought as he set off to rejoin his companions.

He said nothing to Tildy or Gump about Shad Ashley. Perhaps, after all, the Sioux would run him down. Or perhaps he was dead already. Willie thought that unlikely. When had life ever been easy when it could be hard?

After sharing the soldiers' camp that night, Willie and Gump rose early to get the horses saddled. Tildy cooked breakfast for the soldiers in return for a jar of molasses and a rough-drawn map of the Sweetwater basin. When they prepared to ride on, Lieutenant Reed pointed them southeastward through the hills and on to the Red Desert.

"You'll be safe out there," the lieutenant assured them. "No Sioux to trouble you."

"Thanks," Willie said as he tied the reins of the packhorse behind his saddle. "Gump, you leading?"

"Sure," the old-timer grumbled.

Gump headed southward, across the narrow river, and along into the hills. Once out of view of the soldiers, he swung back toward the river, though.

"Lose your way, Gump?" Willie asked.

"Found it," Gump answered. "That lieutenant only said what his colonel told him to. If he'd really wanted us south, he would've sent along an escort to make sure we went that way. He knows what we're doin'."

"And what's that?" Tildy asked.

"Headin' for Saint Mary's Station," Gump explained. "There we can decide our route."

"If the Sioux don't settle it first," Willie remarked.

"You know the Sioux, do you, Wil?" Gump asked, grinning.

"I know 'em some," Willie growled. "Enough to keep clear of 'em."

"Oh?" Tildy asked.

"I came up into the Bighorn country after the war was over," Willie explained. "Been up to Kansas with some cattle. Had a disagreement of sorts, you might say. That was my first trip into the high country. I won't soon forget it."

"What happened?" Tildy asked.

"Decided to try my hand at mining," Willie began. "They said a man could get rich up in Montana, and the way there was up the Bozeman Trail. This is, the Sioux didn't take to having white men drag wagons through their best hunting ground."

"*Their* ground?" Gump cried. "That country belonged to the Crows 'fore the Sioux got themselves pushed into it."

"Well, I heard that myself," Willie admitted, "but that didn't change Red Cloud's attitude. He wasn't fond of whites anyway, from what I could tell, but at first he didn't kill anybody. He'd have his men round up any trespassers, take their goods, and send 'em on their way. The folks complained, and the army sent soldiers to build forts."

"Why?" Tildy asked. "The land was deeded by treaty, wasn't it? And if nobody got hurt . . ."

"Well, nobody got killed anyway," Willie said, grinning as he recalled. "I was headed up the trail myself, together with a half-Shoshoni guide and another couple of fools, when we happened upon a gang of teamsters heading south. The whole bunch was bone-naked, with nary a gun or a shoe amongst 'em. Red Cloud's way of laughing at 'em, I suppose. They weren't laughing any, though. We gave up some blankets, a bit of food, and a spare rifle. Later outfits started fighting. Some Sioux boys off hunting buffalo got shot, and the whole world caught fire."

"That is ten years past," Gump pointed out. "All that's been settled."

"Ten years is a long time for peace to last in this country," Tildy observed. "Chiefs come and go. Young men dream of war. What was it you said about Vance, Wil? They hurry themselves into men. It's truer in an Indian camp than anywhere."

"Sure is," Gump agreed.

Willie frowned as he remembered how young the bare-chested warriors who'd struck his camp had appeared. Some weren't half-grown. Those who died never would be.

"Look there," Gump called, waving the others to halt.

Willie pulled up and followed the old-timer's pointing finger. A hundred yards in the distance a band of bronze-shouldered riders raced alongside a stampeding herd of buffalo. The hunters drove killing lances into the great beasts' sides, shoulders, and finally their hearts.

"Well, Lieutenant Reed was right about the Sioux being out this way," Willie declared. "Better stay to these hills and give 'em a lot of room. Elsewise, they'll like as not be lancing us."

Gump nodded, and a white-faced Tildy agreed as well. They turned away from the river and crisscrossed the hills instead. Only when the Sioux were safely behind did Gump lead the way back to the Sweetwater.

"Could be others about," Willie warned. "We'd best make camp away from the river tonight."

"We will," Gump responded. "At Saint Mary's Station. It's nigh but ten more miles or so."

"Only ten?" an exhausted Wil Devlin asked. "Why not?"

Tildy sighed and grumbled to herself.

CHAPTER 14

Saint Mary's Station was but the first stop on what seemed an endless march eastward along the Sweetwater River. Soon Willie spotted the deep ruts cut over the years by hundreds of wagons making the slow journey west along the old Oregon Trail. Gump chose the old crossing of the Sweetwater used by those early pioneers to splash across the river to its southern bank.

"I remember this place," Tildy said, frowning. "Johnny Flint drowned here. He fell out of his wagon, and his mother couldn't save him. He was eight."

"Yes," Willie said, nodding. "The very ground speaks of pain and suffering."

On the opposite bank stood a pile of broken china plates and discarded furniture shed to lighten the load. The remains of broken crosses attested that Johnny Flint was not the only one to surrender his life at the crossing.

"Strange we should travel this same road," Tildy told Willie. "It seems like I came this way in another lifetime. I was just a girl myself, hanging on to my father's dream, looking after Vance and telling him everything would be all right when down deep I knew it was less than likely we'd ever see Grandpa."

"You made it then," Willie reminded her. "You will this time, too."

As they continued along the south bank of the Sweetwater, they emerged from the low hills onto a broken plain.

"Down south there's the Green Mountains," Gump explained. "Up north lies the Bighorn country."

"I know," Willie said, nodding grimly as the country took on a familiar look. They'd reached the Sweetwater Flats, that long stretch of empty country haunted by rattlesnakes and prairie ghosts. It put him in mind of the buffalo range back in Texas, of that endless sweeping plain that stretched from Dodge City into Colorado. The distant mountains called to him, whispered promises of solitude and peace. But he turned from them and followed Gump.

"You ever figure where we're headed?" Willie asked when they made camp beside a stage station located at an obscure bend of the river know as Three Crossings.

"Back at Saint Mary's I heard there might be work on the stage line ahead," Gump explained. "They got no need of anybody here, but one fellow said there's a shortage of hands at old Sweetwater Station up ahead."

"How far ahead?" Willie asked.

"Thirty, forty miles maybe. A two-day ride if we take it hard. More with an easy pace."

"And if there's no work there?" Tildy asked.

"Then we might cut south through the Medicine Bow country to Cheyenne," Gump said, frowning. "Or else try the old Bozeman Road up the Powder River."

"All we have in our way's the whole Sioux nation," Willie pointed out. "Me, I say we find ourselves a mountainside, build a cabin, and live as we can. This country's alive with game, and there are fish in the river. Maybe we can run some stock. I've always had a yen to raise horses."

"I can't see you as a rancher myself," Tildy said, laughing at the thought.

"You can't?" he asked. His eyes grew dark, and he wondered how that could be. His father always expected Willie to run the family ranch in Texas. Even as a boy Willie had the knack of handling horses, and he was a fine hand with a rope. He knew men, and he'd led them to war and back. More than once.

"Truth is," Tildy explained, "I'm surprised you've been content to stay with us. You told me yourself you were a wayfarer. Shame there's no longer any need for wagon-train scouts."

"Or buffalo hunters," Gump added.

"Well, we don't need a whole herd, but some fresh meat would be nice," Tildy declared. "How 'bout it? You men figure you could shoot one of those antelope that've been bouncin' past us the past few days?"

"There's fair huntin' in the mountains," Gump said, gazing into the grayish mist that clung that evening to the slopes. "Good season for 'lopes. Care to take my Sharps, Wil?"

"Aren't you coming?" Willie asked.

"It's best I stay and watch the goods," the old-timer insisted.

Willie nodded, knowing it wasn't the goods but Tildy that concerned Gump Barlow. Tildy knew, too, and she scowled.

"Lord, Gump, I can take care of myself," she complained. "Besides, the stage station is just yonder. What manner of fool would ride down on our camp with it right next to the stage depot?"

"Ashley would have," Willie muttered. "Stay, Gump."

The old man returned Tildy's scowl, and she reluctantly surrendered.

So it was that Wil Devlin rode into the Green Mountains early the following morning. He brought along the packhorse to carry the meat from his kill. He hadn't ridden five miles when he spied the first antelope. He then cautiously began to shadow the animal until he spotted the larger herd. Only then did he tie his horses to a nearby cottonwood and set out with Gump's heavy Sharps to down an antelope.

As he crept toward the animals, Willie began to realize that he wasn't the lone hunter after the herd. To his right a slender-shouldered boy of fourteen or so wove through the tall grass. His bare, suntanned shoulders and long raven-colored hair blended naturally into the shadows, and he moved only when a gust of wind set the grass to swaying.

Willie needed no guide to tell him the boy was Sioux. His hair was braided in the style of that tribe, and the boy's high cheekbones reminded Willie of others seen all too close at hand a decade earlier in the Bighorns.

The boy noticed Willie, too. For a long second the two eyed each other with that mixture of fear and suspicion old enemies often share. But there was a more immediate purpose at hand. The antelope would scatter at the first hint of sound. Willie motioned the boy toward a large buck just ahead. The Sioux calmly turned that way, notched an arrow, and closed the distance.

For his part, Willie located a second buck and took aim. One eye continued to keep track of the young Indian, but the antelope merited attention, too. The boy crept closer, then fired his arrow. Once the boy's buck fell, the others sensed the danger. Willie fired, and the entire herd took flight.

Only now did Willie discover the Sioux was not alone. Other arrows flew, and an antiquated flintlock boomed out as well. Three antelope tumbled to the earth, and a dozen Indians rushed out of their hiding places to claim the kills.

Willie took a deep breath, slung the Sharps over one shoulder, and stepped to where his own buck lay. The animal was dead, and Willie made the required throat cut. Then he began dragging the beast toward the waiting horses.

He found his path blocked by a tall, buckskin-clad Sioux.

"I mean you no harm," Willie said, pausing long enough to tap the handle of his pistol and gaze intently into the Indian's eyes. There was no point to starting trouble. There were too many of them, and Willie had no heart for fighting Indians.

"Our land," the Sioux boasted. "Our game."

"My kill," Willie said sourly. "If you had need, I would share it, but you are able hunters. Your eyes have the true aim, and you have meat enough."

"And you?" the warrior demanded. "You hunt for the stagecoach people. You starve the Sioux to feed those who steal our land and shoot our people."

"Not for them," Willie insisted. "For myself, and for two others. I didn't shoot at your people. I could have. Ask that boy over yonder. He saw. Truth is, I've known the plains myself. I've ridden to the buffalo hunt in the old ways, with the Comanches. I don't hunger for your land, and I won't shoot your sons as some would. I, too, mourn the passing of the buffalo, the beaver, the days when a man—well, you know. I read it on your face."

Willie studied the others. Two or three were ready to raise their bows and kill. Another had already collected Willie's horses.

The tall Sioux came closer, then reached out and tore open Willie's shirt. The scars on his chest and ribs, the old saber mark across his belly, and the thin red scars where bullets had been cut all met the Indian's eyes.

"You have fought often," the Sioux said with approval.

"Too often to hunger for more," Willie answered.

"Ah, but it always comes again," the Sioux said sadly. "Take your horses and go, but come no more into these mountains to take our game. Go back to the white man's road."

"I have no heart for that road," Willie said as he dragged the antelope carcass toward the waiting packhorse. "This food will last us many days, though, and I will trouble you no more."

The Sioux muttered to one another, but their leader motioned his men away from the horses. Willie tied the antelope to the packhorse, then mounted his own horse and headed north toward Three Crossings. Soon he was back with Gump and Tildy.

"I've seen it before," Gump commented that night when Willie recounted the incident. "Out here there's a grudging respect among hunters. That Sioux knew he could kill you, but he also knew there'd be a price. A good chief rarely risks a man to kill another. If they'd come upon you unprepared—well, that might well be different."

"Even so, they're pretty far south this summer," Willie observed. "We may well run across others."

"Sure," Gump grumbled. "The lieutenant warned as much. Guess maybe sometimes my old head's too hard for my own good."

"Maybe," Willie said, grinning. "But I didn't much want to cross that Red Desert again myself."

Those next three days Willie felt the eyes of Sioux scouts follow as they snaked their way east along the Sweetwater. Just past Split Rock, a famous Oregon Trail landmark, they came upon a wagon surrounded by three arrow-pierced bodies.

"Looks like those Sioux aren't friendly to everyone," Tildy said, turning away.

"Well, I'd guess whoever did this, it wasn't Sioux," Willie said, prying an arrow from the side of the empty wagon. "No markings on the arrow shaft. Whoever did the scalping made a mess of it, too. More likely there are some raiders about who want folks to believe Indians did it."

"He's right," Gump said, taking a shovel from the packhorse and scratching out a grave for the dead teamsters. "We'll report it to the stage station. They'll wire the army."

"Looks like we've found more trouble," Willie said, frowning as he pushed the wagon off the trail. "It seems to follow me."

"Us," Tildy objected. "It follows us."

Willie nodded.

After reporting the dead teamsters at Split Rock Station, Gump led the way across the river and on to a great gap in a sandstone ridge.

"Devil's Gap," Tildy declared, pointing to it excitedly.

"Devil's Gate," Gump corrected her. "Ever hear the story?"

"A long time ago," Tildy said. "Our scout told us. Some kind of she-wolf was gobbling Cheyenne children, I think."

"Legend's Shoshoni," Willie whispered, staring at the place with rare apprehension. "It's a place of strong spirits."

"How'd you come to know that?" Gump asked.

"I was told of it once by a Shoshoni girl," Willie explained. "I didn't feel it then, but I sure do now. There are safer places to make camp, Gump."

"Nonsense," Gump objected. "No Indian in his right mind comes near to this place."

"Why?" Tildy asked.

"Because it's here the devil went back into the mountains," Gump explained. "And if he ever comes back to the plain, this is the gate he'll use."

That night, as they cooked antelope steaks over a sparse fire, Tildy pleaded to hear the tale again. Gump grinned and told his version.

"Was in the old days, long before the horse, when the Shoshonis hunted the big-nosed cows with long spears. One day they felt the earth shake. They ran from the mountains as this giant devil-beast came to life before their very eyes. He marched around stomping the life out of anyone and anything he could. He had the dark eye, and the medicine chiefs knew he carried the bad spirits inside him. The warriors banded together and danced. They prayed for strength. The sky spirits sent great blasts of lightning to show them the beast. The warrior spirits gave strength to the spear arms. Soon the Shoshonis began to torment the beast with spears and drive it from their camps.

"The beast thundered and shook the earth with its tormented feet, but there was no escape. The mountains blocked its path. Then, raising its great long nose in a terrible howl, it smashed through the mountain itself, leaving the gap you see. Now it can never return to earth save by that single gate."

"I remember now," Tildy said, rubbing a tear from her

eye. "Vance loved those old stories. He used to burrow his way into my side and beg to stay with me lest some monster eat him in his sleep. It was the only time he ever showed fear. Later, when we rolled along the trail, I recall the wheels bounced me near out the back a dozen times. Vance would crash against the barrels sometimes. A ten pound sack of potatoes nearly crushed the life out of him once. He'd wince with pain and laugh it off."

"He was good company on the trail," Willie noted. "I never knew a boy who could stir up so much mischief, either."

"Lord, Wil, I miss him so," Tildy said, sobbing on his shoulder. "He was the only real family I ever had."

"It's only natural to feel the hurt," Willie told her. "I feel the sting myself."

"He was my brother," she said, coughing.

"I had younger brothers myself," Willie said, shuddering as the recollection nearly choked him. "Stephen died when I was eight. He wasn't very big. He caught fever, and the wind just carried him off."

"And the others?" Tildy asked.

"James," Willie said, trembling. Even now the image of the lanky fourteen-year-old dismounting a horse tortured Willie's memory. "When I left for the war, he was a whisper of a boy, hardly tall enough for his head to top the middle rail of a fence. I got back to find him near grown, and changed. I wanted to hear his prayers, listen to his dreams, but I'd been gone too long. We were strangers."

"Is he alive?"

"I don't even know," Willie said, holding her tightly. "It doesn't matter, I suppose. I'm dead to all that. I have been for more than ten years."

"But you still feel for all those places . . . and people. You carry the locket with the yellow-haired girl's likeness."

"Yes," he confessed, "but she's a world away, too."

"I'm not," Tildy told him. "I'm right here beside you."

"I know," he said, shivering as a sudden chill assailed

him. Deep inside, a voice whispered, "For how long?" Willie tried not to hear it. He needed to feel close to somebody just then, longed to belong as much as Tildy did. Theirs, after all, was a partnership born out of need, forged in the deep pits built by loneliness and despair.

"Best catch some sleep soon," Gump urged as he kicked off his boots and climbed into his blankets.

Willie nodded, then placed another log on the dying embers of the campfire. There was something menacing about that place, and he wanted the fire's warmth to stave off an encroaching icy-fingered terror.

"We'll pass Independence Rock tomorrow," Tildy whispered. "And then we'll camp at Sweetwater Station. It'll be the end of our wayfarin', Wil."

"Yes," he said, managing a smile. "And who knows? Maybe it will be the beginning of something better."

"I hope so," she whispered.

"Me, too," Willie said.

And as he pulled the blanket over him a few minutes later and gazed at the flickering pinpoints of light overhead, he prayed better days would greet them. He needed a time of peace. He ached for it.

CHAPTER 15

They set out early the next morning for Sweetwater Station. As he passed the ruts of thousands of pioneer wagons, Willie couldn't help envisioning the cavalcade of emigrants who had once crossed the plain bound for a new start in the West. Well, he was headed east, and he hoped there might be something waiting there.

As they continued, Willie saw the country had changed. No longer were wagon camps spread out along the river. Now fledgling ranches sprang up here and there. Cattle and horses grazed where buffalo once roamed. There was not, in fact, a single buffalo to be seen.

Pity those Sioux, Willie thought. Their sun's setting fast. Civilization's creeping closer, and it's arrival spells the end of the wild, free days of the Plains tribes.

Toward late afternoon they approached the great inverted bowl that was known as Independence Rock. Tildy begged her companions to stop.

"My name's scrawled on that rock," she declared. "Vance's initials, too. I cut 'em into the rock myself. Can't we look for 'em?"

"Why?" Willie asked. "You figure you could find 'em up there? I've seen it myself, Tildy. There must be a thousand names scribbled there. Some wash away when the snows melt. You might find it, but you might just be disappointed."

"Probably," she admitted. "But I wanted to know Vance would be remembered."

"He will be," Willie promised. "But not 'cause his initials are scratched in a rock. He had friends, lots of 'em. That's the way a man is best remembered, don't you think?"

She nodded, and Gump led them on to the station.

It was located in the shadow of Independence Rock, on the north bank of the Sweetwater, where the river began its great bend leading to union with the North Platte. It wasn't much of a station actually, just a collection of pine shacks alongside a small trading post run by Tom Garnett.

"Gump and I'll see about the work," Tildy said as she climbed wearily down from her horse. "Wil, why don't you go over to the trading post and pick up some supplies?"

"What supplies?" he asked. "We surely won't need food if we settle in here."

"I made a list," Tildy said, passing it to him. "Even if we take on work here, I don't plan to live in a bunkhouse with a band of sweaty stable boys and teamsters. We'll fix ourselves a cabin nearby. For that, we'll have to have some tools, and there are other things as well."

"Yes, ma'am," Willie said, shaking his head as he dismounted. It sounded like nonsense. It would take weeks to build a cabin in what spare time was available, and why cook their own meals when food could be had at the station house?

Nevertheless Willie didn't argue. Instead he made his way to Garnett's and passed the list to a bewhiskered fellow of forty or so standing behind a counter.

"Name's Tom Garnett," the trader said, taking both the list and Willie's hand at the same time, "You're new 'round here."

"I am," Willie admitted.

"Plan to stay long?" Garnett asked.

"Depends on whether I can find work."

"It's here to be found," Garnett said, examining the list. "Especially if you've got a strong back and don't mind long hours."

"That's true enough," a slender-shouldered youngster said as he swept a cloud of dust out the door.

"Boy, long as you're over that way, grab a five pound sack of flour, will you?" Garnett asked.

The boy hurried to do just that. His unkempt blond hair and wayward smile halted Willie in his tracks. There was something vaguely familiar about the boy.

"Wil?" the youngster asked as he heaved the flour onto the counter. "Wil Devlin? That you?"

Willie gripped the counter and examined the face. It belonged to a boy of fourteen or so, Willie judged. There were a few dark hairs sprouting on opposite sides of the boy's upper lip, and an annoying crackle beset his voice.

"It's me, Pat Nolan," the boy explained. "From Bonner's. Remember? I helped with the horses."

"Sure," Willie said, gripping the young man's hand. "You've grown some, and I wasn't expecting you so far east of there."

"Well, some fellows burned out the place," Pat explained. "Mr. Wheaton sent some fellows out from Cheyenne to help rebuild. The mines were playin' out, too. Wasn't enough work to keep everybody busy, so I headed out here with Don Barker."

"Barker's here, too?"

"For now," Pat said, leading Willie aside a moment. "We got plans to run some horses a bit west o' here. Mr. Garnett doesn't know, so I'd appreciate you not mentionin' it. He can find another boy to help out easy enough. There's more'n a few driftin' through these hills."

"I'll keep your secret," Willie promised.

"Then I'd best get back to my work," Pat declared, hurrying to collect the remainder of Willie's supplies as Garnett read off each item.

"You know that lad?" Garnett asked when Pat trotted out to a storehouse to fetch a timber saw.

"Worked with him awhile," Willie explained.

"A good enough worker, but a touch dream-struck," Garnett said, chuckling. "Always talkin' about roundin' up wild horses and sellin' 'em hereabouts."

"What's so strange about that?" Willie asked. "Isn't there a market for horses in this country?"

"Sure, but a slip of a boy like that's no match for a range mustang."

He might be, Willie thought, if he learned the right way to go about it.

When the last of the supplies were neatly stacked on Garnett's counter, the trader added up the charges, and Willie paid the sum. Pat then helped carry the supplies to the packhorses.

"That's Gump Barlow's horse," Pat observed as he set a load down beside the animals. "And that's one of Miz Tildy's blankets. You ride in with them, did you?"

"Sure did," Willie said. "They'll be glad to see you, Pat."

"And is Vance along? I could sure do with some good company. I been sleepin' out back with Mr. Garnett's dog. That Vance owes me four bits, and he never did teach me that one chord on his mouth organ."

"Here," Willie said, handing Pat half a dollar. "From Vance."

"Where is he?" Pat asked, frowning as Willie's smile faded.

"Well," Willie explained, "you told me about Ashley burning the station. We had a run-in with him, too. Vance—well, he didn't have the sense to stay where it was safe. You know how he was forever running out to help! He . . ."

"Yeah," Pat said, dropping his chin onto his chest. "Been a lot o' dyin' lately. There's talk worse's still to come, too. The Sioux've been raidin' some of the new ranches north o' the Sweetwater."

"It's their country," Willie muttered. "You got to expect 'em to fight for it. They did once before."

Garnett appeared with a box of supplies and set it beside the rest.

"I thought maybe you'd been through this country before," the trader said. "Don't see many headin' east. I heard what you said about the Sioux. We had some soldiers from General Crook's outfit through here talkin' 'bout a fall campaign to drive the hostiles back to their reservations."

"What?" Willie asked.

"Whole Bighorn country's alive with 'em. They keep to the Dakota reservation in winter, then ride out first thaw to hunt. And to kill whites, some say. Government plans to end that. Red Cloud agreed to set up agencies to the east after the Powder River War. Crook plans to help those Indians back home."

"But there's a treaty," Willie objected. "I remembered. The Sioux twice liked to killed me in the Bighorns. I paid awful close attention to the treaty. Those Indians didn't give up their country. It's all set up like a hunting reserve for 'em."

"That's not how the government sees it," Garnett explained. "Ten years is a long time to lay out half a territory for a band or two of bucks to chase buffalo across. That land's needed for settlers. The Black Hills are to be bought, too. That'll move the Sioux into the Badlands where they can harm nobody. Good riddance! Sioux, Cheyenne, Arapaho—the whole lot's best run elsewhere, and Crook's makin' plans to do just that."

"Then he'll find himself in a whale of a fix," Willie grumbled. "Those Indians aren't about to give up their best hunting grounds. No wonder they're crowding the Sweetwater. They must've heard."

"Well, never you worry yourself with 'em," Garnett advised. "General Crook'll settle accounts with the Sioux soon enough."

Garnett then led Pat back to the trading post, and Willie

sat beside the supplies and fumed. It was the same old pattern. Make promises, kill off the game, then hound a tribe till there was nothing left of it. Hadn't Custer done it to the Cheyenne, and the Kiowas before that? Mackenzie finished the Comanches. Now it was Crook's turn to ride down the Sioux.

Will gazed at the setting sun and shook his head.

"Why the frown?" Tildy called from the station house. "Wil, look who's here!"

Don Barker stepped to the door, and Willie returned the big man's nod. Barker was as fine a freight guard as any in the West, and a good friend when the fighting was tight and deadly. The two of them had outfought the Murphy brothers three times and finally seen them buried.

"Tildy here says you've got your eye out for work," Barker said, bounding across the open space toward the hitching racks where Willie stood beside the tethered horses. "Well, I've been lookin' for just this sort of outfit."

"He wants to run horses," Tildy explained. "Isn't that what you mentioned yourself not a week ago?"

"Pat explained it to me," Willie said, turning Tildy toward the shaggy-haired boy who stood in Garnett's doorway. Tildy's eyes began to water, and she raced to greet her brother's friend with outstretched arms.

"Well, now you know, what do you think?" Barker asked.

"We'd need a place to operate," Willie said. "And money for rope and wood, harness and . . ."

"I've got a ranch already," Barker explained. "My sister's husband owns the place. They headed to Cheyenne when the Sioux got active, and I've got the place all to myself."

"It'd take a crew, too," Willie pointed out. "Two men won't trap many mustangs."

"Sure, Wil, but we can settle all that later. Right now why don't we get this gear stowed away in the bunkhouse? I shot some prairie hens for supper, and Tildy's promised to bake biscuits. Lord, my mouth is ready for one of those flaky little things! I don't miss Gump's grumblin' or Pop's howlin', but I sure do long for Tildy's cookin' and that soft guitar music those Mexican boys played over at the stable."

"What became of them?" Willie asked.

"Shot down by Shadrack Ashley," Barker said, grinding his teeth. "As Vance was, I understand. That's hard news indeed. That was one fine boy! Ashley's got a lot to answer for, and I sure was glad when Tildy said that skunk was dead."

"Sure," Willie muttered, shifting his weight nervously.

Tildy then returned with Pat in hand, followed by Tom Garnett. Inside, the other station hands and Martin Freeman, the stationmaster, anxiously hovered near the table as Tildy began preparing supper.

"You tell him about the horses, Don?" Pat asked, settling in between the older men. "Well?"

"I was goin' to," Barker said, clamping a hand over Pat's mouth. "Wil, you wouldn't believe the stock roamin' free out there. Some're strays from emigrant trains. There are Crow and Sioux war ponies, the one run off by the other. Cavalry mounts, too, not to mention all manner of mixes from the lot. A good horse can fetch up to a hundred dollars these days. A bad one goes for twenty-five and up. I figure it's better'n minin' for gold."

"So how would I figure in?" Willie asked.

"I need a steady man to help with the crew for one thing. I need a man who knows horses second. And most of all, I need somebody I can trust if we find ourselves in a tough spot. We'll have an outfit with boys like Pat. I know a young wrangler over at the Cross Timbers Ranch name of Tim Phipps. He's a good one, too, but he's only sixteen. Others'll sign on as word gets out."

"I don't know about all these youngsters," Willie said, frowning. "They're good enough company, Don, but you wind up burying so many of 'em."

"Most of these kids'd starve without the work. Or take up stealin'. Wil, a week o' good grub and fine company's more'n most have to look forward to. Ought to be some good in a man's life before he turns in his chips."

"I suppose," Willie grumbled.

Barker then produced a map and located the ranch for Willie. Next they marked the box canyons and hollows where horses could best be trapped. But when Tildy arrived with dinner, they postponed the talk for a time.

Willie, tired as he was of antelope and pork, gobbled the prairie hen with true passion. The biscuits were equally delicious.

"You got yourself a job as a cook for as long as you like, Tildy," Freeman declared. "Start tomorrow."

"Depends. I might have a better offer," she said, turning to Willie and Barker. "Well?"

"We best hire her," Willie urged his new partner. "We'll need a good cook, and she's a fair shot as well."

"And if need be, I can lance your boils for you, Don Barker," she added to the amusement of the others.

"I better hire her," Barker declared. "I think that was a threat."

The table rocked with laughter again. Then Pat Nolan produced his mouth organ and serenaded the weary station hands with motley tunes.

"Gump?" Willie asked next.

"I'm feelin' a bit old for such doin's," Gump explained.

"We have hands to run down the horses," Barker replied. "We need a man to keep camp, though."

"Tildy can do that," Gump argued. "I'd only be a bother."

"I'll need help at the station," Freeman interjected. "I could sure use a steady man, Gump."

"Then you got one," the old-timer said. "I'll miss Tildy's grub, but I can cook some myself. And this is no place for the two of you, Wil. Take good care of her, hear? I learn otherwise, and you'll see I'm not as old as you judge."

"I'll keep that in mind," Willie said, forcing a grin onto

his face. "Tildy, Gump, I didn't mean to break up our partnership. It's just . . ."

"That this is what you really want to do," Tildy said, clutching his hand. "I understand, Wil. It's that fresh start you've spoken of. Well, I want one, too."

"Then it's settled?" Willie asked

"When do we leave?" Pat asked, setting aside his mouth organ a moment. "Tell me."

"Day after tomorrow all right?" Barker asked. "Take a bit of time to collect everything we need."

"Sounds fine," Willie said, turning to Tildy. She nodded her agreement, and Pat howled.

"I been savin' this awhile," Gump said, drawing out a brandy flask. He poured a small quantity of the smoky liquid in glasses and passed them around the table. Pat raised his first, and the others matched the toast.

"To a venture ably begun," Barker called.

"Amen," Gump added.

The others shouted their agreement, and Willie swallowed his in a single gulp. He then escorted Tildy outside, and they gazed together at the single star shining over the Green Mountains.

"Evening star," Willie declared. "The Comanches thought it good luck for me."

"For us, too," she whispered. "Or so I hope."

"Me, too," he said as he drew her near. "Me, too."

CHAPTER 16

The next morning Don Barker conducted Willie and Tildy Bonner to the SC Ranch.

"SC for Sweetwater Crossing," Barker explained. The place, after all, bounded the old Oregon Trail crossing. To call it a ranch required a strong imagination. There was a dugout cabin of sorts and three empty corrals made of weathered cottonwood rails. Barker waved his companions toward the dugout, then set off to collect hands for the range crew.

Pat Nolan escorted Tim Phipps in a bit after noon. Underfed and not much bigger than Pat, young Phipps rode with a self-assuredness that caught Willie's eye at once. The sixteen-year-old's quiet manner was a marked contrast to Pat's constant jabbering.

Tildy motioned the two boys to a collection of ash slats and dusty blankets she had cleared from the cabin.

"See if you can resurrect two beds from that mess," she suggested.

"Sure, Tildy," Pat said, slapping a frayed blanket so hard that a cloud of dust swallowed both of the amber-haired teenagers.

"Not me," Tim announced, retreating ten yards. "I'd rather sleep on the roof."

Tildy smiled, and Willie could tell the remark had endeared the youngster to her.

"Looks like you've found some more motherin' for me to do," she complained to Willie. He knew, though, she didn't mean it. Soon she was clipping Tim Phipps's stringy hair and bossing Pat around like the foreman of a rail gang.

Barker returned at suppertime with a pair of lanky brothers, the Redmonds. Both appeared somewhat seedy, but Willie observed their horses were well cared for, and they were polite toward Tildy.

"We've had a time of it findin' work," Ned, the younger one, explained. "Hunted buffs down in Kansas till that played out. Been doin' our best to dodge Sioux Indians and keep from starvin'."

Curly, the older one at close to thirty, nodded. The name brought a laugh from Pat Nolan. Curly Redmond was as bald as a walnut.

"Used to have long red hair, though," Ned explained. "Sure will be a disappointment one of these days when our luck turns, and some Sioux takes a scalpin' knife to him."

Even Tim Phipps grinned at the thought.

The last to join the company rode in just as Tildy placed a platter of biscuits on the table. Willie glanced outside through the narrow slit of a window in time to spy a buffalo hide topped by a broad-brimmed leather hat stepping toward the door. Aside from a mane of long, unkempt black hair, the figure seemed to have neither face, arms, nor feet.

"This the SC Ranch?" a scratchy voice called.

"It is," Barker replied, swinging open the door.

The newcomer pulled off his hat and shed the buffalo hide. Underneath was a skeleton-thin figure dressed in buckskin trousers and coarse cotton shirt open to the breastbone. On his feet were a well-worn pair of beaded moccasins.

"I'm Colter, aged sixteen and a bit more," the newcomer declared, forcing his voice into a deeper tone than was natural.

"Got a Christian name?" Tildy asked, examining the young man with a critical eye.

"No," he answered. "I never been exactly baptized or such. Been with my papa, tradin' goods with the Indians since I was born. That was in the Red River country, Minnesota. Papa took ill a month back, and I buried him on the Medicine Bow."

"He's called Chip," Pat explained. "He brought in some goods for Mr. Garnett."

"Short for Chippewa," the boy said.

"You part Indian?" Ned Redmond asked.

"Part everything," Chip said, stone-faced. "Hardly knew my mama, and Papa didn't talk much 'bout her. But I hear you plan to run down range ponies, and I'm as good a hand at findin' em as you'll ever see."

"That right?" Barker asked, grinning.

"Try me," Chip suggested. "I don't ask you to pay me a nickel 'fore I find you some horses. If we run across trouble you'll find me steady. I've got a big bore Sharps tied across my saddle, and I speak passable most every tongue 'tween here and Canada."

"Sixteen, you say?" Willie asked, laughing to himself. "You can't be more than five feet in boots!"

"I was five when the Santee Sioux killed Mama," Chip said without flinching. "That was in sixty-four. Out here doesn't do a man much good to be tall. Makes him a bigger target. While back I cut a few inches off myself to reduce the odds, so to speak."

"Oh?" Tildy asked, smiling.

"Don't get him started with stories," Pat warned. "We'll still be at it when the biscuits're stone cold."

"Why don't you sit yourself down, Chippewa Colter," Tildy said, pointing out an empty chair. "I've had a pork pie bakin', and you look in need of a meal."

"Need a job worse," Chip said, making no move toward the table.

"We could run across real trouble where we're going,"

Willie said, frowning. "I'm none too eager to lead a band of youngsters to their deaths."

"I seen folks scalped, men ridden down by buffalo, a whole village dead o' pox, and a few fellows got themselves eaten up by their partners high up in the Rockies," Chip said, gazing intently into Willie's eyes. "You figure to take me a worse place?"

"Maybe," Willie said. "I never found a gentle trail yet."

"Well, don't you worry, mister. I run real fast, too."

"Wil?" Barker asked.

"I don't see how we can do without him," Willie replied. "He lies better than Pat, he's got more hair than Curly, smells worse than Ned, and he's skinnier than Tim."

"And hungrier'n sin, beggin' your pardon, ma'am," Chip said, pulling the chair over and sitting at the table. "Biscuit?"

Chip Colter ate more than anyone Willie had ever seen. Tildy wound up frying some bacon and shoveling an extra platter of biscuits in and out of the Dutch oven. Chip returned the favor by entertaining the others with tales of his wanderings.

"You fellows know the Yellowstone country?" Chip asked. When the others shook their heads, the youngster beamed a giant smile. "Strange place full o' spirits. There's a valley up there full o' bubblin' mud. Smells bad as the Laramie stinks, or worse. There's fountains o' steam that shoot a hundred feet straight into the air, and hot springs where you can take a bath in the middle o' winter, with snow fallin' thick as goose feathers.

"Best part, though," Chip continued, "is where the water bubbles up through these white mounds. Papa called 'em 'talkin' rocks', 'cause he said the old people listen to 'em and know what's bound to happen. Strange place, that. I plan to get back up there one day if the Sioux settle down. Nowadays they'd as soon scalp a white man as look at him, I hear. I'm not all white, mind, but I got an awful lot o' hair on my head. Look mighty good on a lodge pole, don't you think?"

"Not as pretty as mine, though," Pat argued. In no time the boys were arguing the merits of hair with Curly Redmond. Willie grinned, sat beside Tildy, and braided a rawhide lariat. For the first time since leaving Rock Creek, he saw the pain leave her face.

Early the next morning Willie and Don Barker had the outfit busy gathering provisions, saddling horses, and throwing ropes over the corral posts. Ned Redmond had the knack for dropping a loop over whatever he chose, and he twice roped Pat Nolan. Pat, though he was a good hand with the horses, was hopeless with a rope.

Tim Phipps, on the other hand, knew ranch work. Barker had been right to sign the youngster on. What Tim lacked in size he made up for with concentration. What's more, he worked as well on horseback as Don Barker or even Willie himself.

Curly lacked his brother's skill, but the elder Redmond never seemed to tire. He was strong as an ox, too, and Willie welcomed that.

The last and strangest member of the crew was Chip Colter. The dark-haired boy disdained the lariat.

"I'll find you the ponies," Chip explained. "I'll gentle 'em. I won't drag 'em into some corral."

"Can't gentle what's running free on the plains," Willie pointed out.

"There'll be enough ropers," Ned declared. "I'll bet he puts himself to good use."

Something in Chip's eyes told Willie Ned was right.

An hour short of midday Don Barker tied the provisions onto three packhorses and ordered the crew to mount up. Barker led the way out onto the windswept plain, with Chip and the Redmonds close behind. Pat and Tim followed. Willie brought up the rear.

For close to three hours, no one so much as spotted a horse's tail. Then Chip motioned toward the left and set off at a half gallop.

Willie was mystified by the boy's sudden charge. Then a flash of white mane on the far hillside explained it.

"Horses!" Pat cried, turning toward the white.

"Oh, Lord," Willie groaned as the crew headed in five directions. Barker managed to hold the pack animals in check. Willie, meanwhile, prepared to circle around and cut off the escape path of the ponies.

In his heart, Willie regretted throwing a rope over a range pony as much as Chip Colter. Those horses, the spawn of cavalry steeds and tribal war ponies, were the last free creatures on earth. Strong of heart, clever of foot, and possessed of the bold daring common to all old warriors, the animals were somehow magical. Capturing and breaking them to saddle was business, though . . . survival. It offered a man a better future.

Willie spotted Pat Nolan trying without success to corner a spotted stallion in a boulder-strewn gully. Racing over, Willie tossed his lariat over the animal's neck, then drew the horse alongside as the stallion snorted and fought to catch its breath.

"Here, Pat," Willie called, waiting for the youngster to drop a loop over the stallion. Once secured, Willie started to hand over his lariat. The stallion, sensing a slackening of the lariat's grip on its throat, reared into the air and made a break for the plain. Pat, gripping the rope with all his might, was lifted bodily out of the saddle and bounced along the ground fifty feet or so before Willie regained control of the rebellious horse.

"Fine ride, Pat!" Tim Phipps called as he led over a midnight-black pony.

"Not so fine," Pat said, shaking off the dust and rubbing his bottom. Sandstone and sagebrush had torn a square-foot gap in his trousers. Even Willie laughed.

Young Phipps took charge of the spotted stallion and the reddening boy while Willie set off after the white mare that had first drawn their attention.

The white ran with the clouds, and Willie only managed to trap the beast by turning circles eastward. Finally he slapped his mount into a gallop and closed on the horse like an eagle diving from above. The mare, weary from the chase, barely moved.

Willie also roped a pair of mustang mares before the remaining horses broke past the weary wranglers and escaped onto the distant range. In all, though, the outfit had roped a dozen promising ponies, including the graceful white and a trio of stubborn stallions.

"Now the fun begins, eh?" Ned asked. "Got to break 'em to saddle."

"Lord, I like to have my hands peeled and my thumbs rubbed off workin' fool horses!" Tim lamented. "Got to be crazed comin' over with you fellows so I can do it all over again."

"Not crazed," Pat objected. "Just hungry. When you get real tired and hurt worse, just remember Tildy's biscuits. Shoot, I can almost forget my backside's rubbed raw when I do that!"

Willie laughed, and Pat flashed a good-natured grin. Pat might not be much of a wrangler, but he was good for the spirit, Willie decided. And once the boy grew a bit and learned to handle a rope, he'd do.

They made camp that night at a shallow creek two miles south of the Sweetwater. Once the horses were securely tied to stout cottonwoods, the weary horsemen peeled off their clothes and jumped into the water. The cool creek breathed new life into each of them, but it also betrayed just how small and thin and pale the younger members of the outfit were.

"I do believe we've taken on a crew of babes," Barker told Willie. "That Colter boy's no sixteen!"

"Doesn't matter," Willie declared. "He's got a nose for finding horses, and he's steady enough. As for Phipps, you said yourself he's as good a hand as there is around. Both the Redmonds together didn't put in half the day that boy did. As for Pat, once I get some tree moss on his backside, and we stitch him some new britches, he'll live."

Barker nodded, grinned, then found himself attacked by the three boys and dragged into the creek for an impassioned scrubbing. The youngsters noted the multiple bullet scars on Willie's chest and back, not to mention the jagged scar on his thigh. They seemed respectful of the man who had survived such violence, especially when Pat stretched the tale of Willie's battle with the Murphy brothers into a minor legend.

As the sun set, Chip Colter stirred a skillet of beans and pork, dropping in a bit of this and that for seasoning. A wonderful aroma rose, and Willie was amazed to find the food more than a little pleasing.

"What else can you do, Chip?" Willie asked as he emptied his bowl.

"What you need?" Chip asked.

"Ever heal a twisted soul?" Willie asked, turning somber. "Patch a tear in a man's heart?"

"I saw Pat," Chip said, studying the older man closely. "You know medicine ways yourself. Only the spirits can cure."

"Ever see a horse gentled in the old way?" Willie asked. "No whip or rope's end. Just the man and the animal and a lot of patience."

"Once or twice. Never by a yellow-haired man."

"Watch tomorrow," Willie urged. "Care to lend a hand?"

"You've done it before," Chip said, nodding respectfully. "I read it in your eyes. It's a power, they say. How does a man like that end up in the Sweetwater Flats?"

"The wind blows a man without roots most anywhere."

"Yes, it does," Chip agreed. The boy then set off for the warmth of the campfire. Pat was playing a lively tune on the mouth organ, and the Redmonds were singing a bawdy lyric.

He's a strange boy, Willie thought to himself. Reminds me of someone. Willie hoped fate would have kinder days in store for Chippewa Colter than for the nimble-footed boy who had chased Ellen Cobb through the Brazos shallows.

CHAPTER 17

While the others continued to chase down range ponies, Willie began working the wild horses into saddle mounts. Others might have begun with a willow switch and a bull-whip. Willie fashioned a halter, slipped it over the reluctant white mare's nose, past bared teeth, and secured the animal to a nearby willow tree.

"Well, girl?" he then asked as he conducted the mare around the tree. "Gettin' used to me, aren't you? Smell that smoke in my hair, the trail dust and grit ground into my hide? Get used to it. We'll soon be old friends."

The mare seemed unconvinced. Willie's touch brought the animal's feet to life; she began stomping the ground and kicking out at the air in protest.

"Don't fight me, girl," Willie urged. "I'm like the wind and the clouds, you know. There's nothing to me."

The real work commenced when the wranglers returned to the SC Ranch. While others tugged and whipped their ponies into submission, Willie continued to work his animals with the same quiet persuasion learned so long ago in old Yellow Shirt's Comanche camps. Soon a firm hand and a lot of patience began to take hold. The horses rebelled less and less. Willie finally managed to tie a blanket full of pine logs and small rocks on the mare. The horse did its best to shake loose of the burden, but the ropes held.

"So, it's time we put me to the test, isn't it?" Willie asked one particularly bright morning. "Will you give me your heart, Whitey? Eh?"

Willie then cut loose the burden and replaced it with a saddle. In another moment he placed his toe in a stirrup and mounted the mare. The horse reacted instantly, bucking and dipping a shoulder so as to dislodge its rider. At first the mare whined and stomped angrily. By and by the horse settled, and Willie stroked the animal's white mane and whispered an old Comanche song.

"Never thought you'd bring her 'round," Pat Nolan observed as Willie rode briskly around the corral.

"Not that way, anyhow," Tim agreed. "Grandpa used to give 'em a good tarrin' if they'd buck."

"Ruins 'em," Willie declared. "A horse like this one'll run all the way to tomorrow for you, but not if all the spirit's been whipped out of her."

The boys nodded and tempered their own approach. Chip Colter smiled approvingly.

"Yes," the raven-haired youngster told Willie, "you've been a time with the tribes yourself. You know the old ways. The Sioux would take a pony to the river, drown him some if he fought too much. I've seen the Crows speak to a pony and make its heart one with its rider."

"Comanches, too," Willie whispered. "It's the best way."

Soon Willie found himself teaching the others. It was pure pleasure to watch little Pat Nolan clinging to the back of a cavorting mustang.

"Talk to him, Pat!" Willie urged. "Tell him you mean to keep at it till he settles down."

"I been doin' that," Pat answered. "He just isn't any too convinced!"

Each evening Willie wearily took to his bed. Old aches began to make themselves known again, and new ones exacted a price. But though he began to smell of sweat and horseflesh and look a little like some old miner's mule that'd been ridden too hard, the work purged him of the nightmares of recent memory. And when the fatigue vexed him most, Tildy was there to offer comfort and sympathy.

In mid-July Gump Barlow paid them a visit. Willie showed the old-timer around the place, pointed out a corral of prancing ponies, and introduced the Redmonds and Chip.

"Seems to me you've close to got yourselves a real ranch here," Gump declared. "But you can't live forever in that dugout. Sure, it's fine for wranglers and cow ponies, but it's time Tildy had a proper kitchen and a real house."

Willie nodded, then followed Gump to a rise of ground overlooking the river.

"That's where I'd put a house," Gump said, grinning. "Cut some o' those tall pines on yon hills into planks, carve some shingles, and you'd have yourself a fair house. Those boys look fit enough to hold a hammer and a saw. Well?"

"Somebody'd have to keep 'em at the work," Willie insisted. "It'd have to be a man used to long days and boys' ways. Know any fool we could hire on?"

"Just one," Gump said, plunging a thumb into his chest. "Am I hired?"

"Yes," Willie announced, grinning. "Welcome home, Gump."

The old man's arrival brought a glow to Tildy's face, and as the house took shape, she began to speak more and more of the future.

"It's not just a house we're buildin'," she told Willie often. "It's a life. I miss Vance, but we've got Tim and Pat along, not to mention that Chip Colter. Shoot, I'm even gettin' used to Curly and Ned."

As she spoke of planting a garden and sewing curtains for the windows, Willie gazed at the river and recalled that other place, the other yellow-haired girl. Ellen would never be truly forgotten, nor the old dream, either. But perhaps it wasn't lost after all. Maybe the dream was only deferred, and he and Tildy could give it a fresh beginning.

Gump, as true to his word as always, had the Redmonds, Barker, and the boys busy from dawn to dusk hammering boards into place or felling pines and cottonwoods. The sounds of the house coming to life filled Willie with a fresh sense of purpose. He worked the stock with rare love, and the animals responded. Soon word spread of the SC's fine string, and buyers began appearing, cash in hand, to bid on the ponies.

"By September we'll have enough put aside to buy up some cattle, run 'em onto the range out west," Barker declared. "In a year or so we'll all of us be rich."

"I am already," Willie observed. After so many trials and countless miles, he'd found peace.

Early the next morning two wagons splashed across the river. Riding alongside was a tall Georgian, Gordon Statham, who announced he had acquired the acreage just south of the SC.

"Fellow named Garnett said you might sell me some saddle horses," Statham said. "My brother'll be along in a week with some cattle, and I expect to need mounts for a good range crew."

"We got 'em," Willie said, beckoning the newcomer to the corral. "Have a look for yourself."

Statham did just that, and he was pleased with what he found. The Georgian bought six, leaving only the white mare, now heavy with foal, and two spotted mustangs who remained a trifle wild about the edges.

"A fair profit," Barker announced as Statham passed on a stack of bank notes. "But we'd best make another visit to the wilds soon."

"Yes," Willie reluctantly agreed. Once he would have eagerly mounted his horse and led the way. Now he was full of a rare sense of direction, of belonging. He felt no urge to leave Tildy for the lonely campfires of the buffalo range.

The others seemed to feel at home as well. When the house was finally deemed ready for habitation, Don Barker moved into the back room. Tildy took the larger room across from the kitchen, and Willie shared the front room with Gump. The Redmonds and the youngsters remained in the dugout bunkhouse, though around dusk the boys collected in the kitchen to sing and swap tales.

Pat would play his mouth organ, and Chip usually contributed a story of the wild Yellowstone country or perhaps a yarn he'd heard in some Indian camp. Tim Phipps normally sat beside the window, humming along with Pat's eerie melodies or nodding at the story. Occasionally the tales would stretch the truth some, and Tim's eyebrows would rise accordingly.

"Guess that grizzly was big, all right," the boy said when Gump described a bear who'd splintered a miner's cabin with one paw.

"Oh, he was a monster," Gump assured his audience. "You can believe that!"

"Yeah," Tim muttered. "Close to as big as your imagination, Gump. Been any bigger, he could've made that hole in the mountains you told us about."

"Where'd that come from?" Tildy asked, laughing. "Tim? That wasn't you, was it?"

The others eyed the near-silent sixteen-year-old and watched Tim's face take on a shade of pink.

"Isn't natural to believe just everything, you know," Tim told them, straight-faced as ever. "Even a wrangler's got some sense."

Willie looked on as Tildy walked over and wrapped an arm around Tim's thin shoulder. She squeezed the boy till he turned close to blue. He didn't attempt to wriggle free, though, and Willie detected a rare tear in his eye.

"Thank you, Tim," Tildy whispered as she rubbed her own eyes clear of moisture.

"Figure this means we're promised, Wil?" Tim asked, cracking a smile.

"Better not," Willie answered, tapping the barrel of his pistol. "Consider it a sisterly hug."

"That right, Sis?" Tim asked. "Can I call you that?"

Tildy buried her face in her hands and nodded.

"I say somethin' wrong?" Tim asked, turning to the others.

"Wrong?" Willie asked. "I'd say you just set an awful lot of wrong as close to right as it can get."

Tildy nodded, and thenceforth she was "Sis" to all three youngsters. Pat insisted on a hug as well, and the blustery boy turned pinker than Tim. Chip said nothing, but Willie detected a quiver in the youngster's steady hands.

"So, I've got a family again, haven't I?" Tildy asked as Willie walked with her alongside the river. "They're callin' Gump 'Pop', you know."

"I'm just glad they didn't save that for me."

"You? No, they saved you for me, Wil Devlin."

"Oh?"

"I guess maybe we ought to hunt ourselves up a preacher 'fore long. I got three brothers who frown at havin' their sister trifled with. Ever get a good look at that Sharps Chip totes around?"

"A few times," Willie confessed. "Tildy, I know we've spoken of this before, but it's a big leap you're talking about. Mighty deep gorge to cross."

"Not half as big as the hole you've filled," she explained. "I thought the hurt in that hole would swallow me, Wil. We got the house built. Now all that's missin' is a man to share my nights, to see my kids raised."

"Three brothers aren't enough, eh?"

"Not for you, either," she observed. "I watched you gazin' in the back of the Statham's wagon at that herd o' kids. You wouldn't mind havin' a straw-haired boy to teach those old ways to, and I have to find some way o' sharin' the cookin'. You boys show scant signs of hirin' on a girl."

"Most o' the ones who pass through here take to a different trade," Willie observed.

"Then I guess I'll have to grow my own. With your help, that is."

Willie turned and stared at the river sparkling in the moonlight. Was it possible the air could be so crisp, that the world could taste so new and alive?

"You find that preacher," he whispered. "I can't think of a finer way for a man to pass his life."

They embraced, and he felt his heart pound like the thunder of a dozen Yank field pieces. Yes, life tasted sweet, didn't it? Yes, indeed it did!

CHAPTER 18

It was early the next morning when Chip spotted the buffalo.

"Only twenty or so, but I thought they were all dead, sure," the youngster announced excitedly. "A man should grow strong on buffalo meat, shouldn't he, Wil? You know the plains ways. Fish and pork are fine for some, but a man needs to taste the buffalo and know the hunt."

"Gump?" Willie asked, turning to the old-timer.

"Me, I got no heart to hurry the last o' those humpers to their graves," Gump said, sighing. "I seen the trails black with their hundreds. Now they're 'most gone. If you want meat, let's shoot antelope or buy some o' Statham's cows."

"It's not the same," Chip argued.

"No, it's not," Tim said, gazing intently at Willie. "My pa once dropped a buff, but I've scarce seen one. Take us, Wil?"

"Wil?" Pat added.

Willie turned to Barker, who nodded.

"Been a time since I tasted a buff steak myself," Barker pointed out. "Does a man good to try his hand at a new thing now and then."

"If we go, it ought to be done right, in the old way," Willie declared.

"Yes," Chip agreed. "You can teach us?"

"I can," Willie said, gazing at Tildy's reluctant eyes.

"How long will you be gone?" she asked.

"A day, perhaps two at most."

"Well, I guess you best not disappoint 'em," she said. "Just see you dress the meat and strip the hide 'fore you come back. I got no interest in more work."

"Agreed," Willie promised.

And so early that next morning Willie led the way westward, following the path of fresh buffalo chips left beside the Sweetwater. Chippewa Colter, old Sharps big bore tied behind his saddle, took the lead. Willie had Gump's old Sharps, and he led the others. Tim Phipps rode silently behind a jabbering Pat Nolan. Don Barker brought up the rear.

Around midday Chip spotted the buffalo. They were grazing along the river some fifteen miles west of the SC Ranch. Pat immediately raised a whoop and started to charge after the herd. Willie shook his head and led the way toward a nearby hill.

"It's not the way," he explained. "First we camp. Tomorrow we hunt."

It had been fifteen years or more since Willie Delamer rode after buffalo alongside young Red Wolf, the Comanche youth who had been a brother in all ways but blood. Old Yellow Shirt had explained the cycles of life around a campfire the night before, how the life of the tribe flowed from the death of the buffalo, and how the buffalo spirits gave the lives of their brothers to sustain the Comanche.

"We must ask the spirits to give up their brothers," the chief had said. "We must ask that the meat sustain us, that our eyes warn of danger, and that our bow arms hold the true aim."

Willie sat beside a smaller fire toward nightfall speaking those same words. Tim nodded out of respect without really understanding. As for Don Barker, he had lived long enough in the wilds of the Wyoming Territory not to question what another believed.

Afterward, Chip spun a tale of Sioux hunters while Pat played a mournful tune on his mouth organ. Willie spread his blankets away from the others. As he searched the vast plain for the brown clumps that they would hunt at dawn, he recalled that other hunt a lifetime ago.

"So, Ellie, you were right," he whispered. "You said I should find peace, find someone, make a fresh start. She's a good woman, one you'd like. And who knows? Maybe we can build the ranch Papa always dreamed of."

The thought warmed him, and he dreamed that night of Tildy, of how she'd stand with a ribbon in her hair while a preacher read the marrying words from his prayer book. He envisioned the yellow-haired little boys who would sit at his side around the fireplace, listening to the old tales of the Delamers and sharing the winter silence and the July sunshine.

The sun woke him as it broke the far eastern horizon. Willie stretched his arms out to his sides and shook off the predawn stiffness. He felt good, better than he could remember. The buffalo were stirring down on the plain, and Chip already had a fire crackling.

"Tonight we'll have buffalo steaks to chew," he boasted as the others shivered off the morning chill.

"Will, how many you figure we can kill?" Pat asked. "I heard a stage passenger say he saw sixty-five dropped in one stand."

"We'll take two," Willie said, gazing toward the buffalo. "That's meat enough. The others we leave be."

"Two?" Tim asked, clearly disappointed. "I thought we could each of us have a coat from the hides. Would six be so many?"

"Yes," Willie grumbled. "I'd have it so there are buffalo left for your sons to hunt, and their sons after them. Kill 'em all, and there'll come a dreadful punishment of it, I fear."

"You really believe in all those spirits, Wil?" Barker asked.

"I believe what I've seen," Willie answered. "And what I feel." And what I know, he thought.

After eating a quick breakfast of fried bacon and biscuits, washed down by a cup of muddy coffee, Willie organized his outfit. He then led the way along a deep gully until they were no more than fifty feet from the herd. The wind blew the scent of grazing beasts into their nostrils. It was a familiar odor, a scent that troubled Willie some. Always before, dark death had followed. It seemed too fine a morning for that.

"Here," Willie whispered, motioning for young Pat to take Gump's powerful rifle. "Wait for Tim, though. Aim just below the chin, at the chest. Make sure of your aim, too. It should be quick, painless."

Pat nodded. Chip then passed his Sharps to Tim Phipps. The shooters had been chosen earlier. Willie knew Chip would rather lose a toe than miss the shot, and yet he'd suggested young Phipps fire.

"I suppose we could take three," Willie had declared.

"No, two," Chip said sadly. "I've ridden to the hunt before. Besides, Pat couldn't hit a barn with a stick. I'll have my chance."

Chip cradled Willie's Winchester and huddled at the edge of the ravine a few feet from Pat. Don Barker took his station at Tim's side. Willie watched from a few feet closer to the river. His eyes weren't watching the herd, though. They were closed. His thoughts wandered as he touched the faint scar on his wrist. He relived that wild charge from his youth when he'd raced at breakneck speed toward the thundering buffalo, shooting as dust choked his lungs and stung his eyes.

He blinked his eyes and stared back at the others. Pat and Tim studied the grazing animals with serious eyes. There was no boasting, no youthful bravado. They were hunters as Willie had been, as the Comanches were. Willie smiled proudly and waved. Two thundering blasts tore the morning apart.

The first shot, Tim Phipps's, dropped a prowling bull

straightaway. Pat Nolan's ball struck a second bull in the flank. Instantly the herd roared into motion. Even though there were but thirty of the beasts, they shook the ground with their hooves.

"I missed!" Pat cried as he fought to reload the rifle. Chip steadied his Winchester and waited for the wounded bull to stumble past. The rifle barked, and the bull fell forward, dragging his chin along the ground five full steps before pitching forward, dead.

There were no cheers raised. The other buffalo stampeded off along the river, leaving their fallen brothers to the mercy of sharp knives. Willie hurried forward to make the throat cuts, then waved for his companions to bring the horses down.

"Thank you, buffalo spirits, for giving them this hunt," Willie whispered as the others hurried after the horses. "This meat will make us strong, will help these boys grow tall in all the ways that are important."

Soon Barker was skinning the first bull. Tim and Pat worked at weaving cottonwood limbs into a travois to carry the meat. Chip and Willie butchered the second carcass.

Suddenly Willie felt a chill. It was as if a shadow crossed over his brow. He cast aside his knife and stood. Turning to his right, he saw the first one. Others appeared to the left. Three more closed in from behind.

"Wil?" Pat asked nervously.

"Go on with your work," Willie urged. "Don't act nervous."

"But they're . . ."

"I know," Willie mumbled as he stepped carefully toward the nearest one. "Sioux."

The Indians were a mixed lot. Two old, wrinkled men sat atop painted ponies. A younger man, perhaps in his late thirties, rode between them. The others were all young, the eldest perhaps as tall as Chip Colter and not quite so old.

Willie reached down and unbuckled his pistol belt. The gun fell harmlessly at his side. He opened his shirt to show no weapon lurked there. Finally he stopped ten feet from the Indians and raised his hand solemnly.

The younger of the three men pointed at the slain buffalo and shouted angrily. His hands moved back and forth wildly, and the words flew like barbed arrows, each aimed at Willie's heart.

Willie then felt a hand on his shoulder. Chip Colter, bared to the waist, stepped forward. He spoke slowly, calmly, to the Sioux. The Indian answered harshly.

"He says we kill the buffalo, starve his people," Chip said soberly. "He says the bones of the buffalo stain the prairies white."

"He's right enough," Willie said, staring into the Indian's eyes. "But I'm no hide hunter! We need meat, too. The buffalo spirit doesn't just answer the prayers of the Sioux. We come, in the old way, seeking the strength the buffalo spirits give to the strong of heart. It's right the young should learn the old ways. I come to teach them!"

Chip started to translate, but Willie saw the words had been understood well enough. There was something familiar in the Sioux's cold glare, and Willie realized it was the same Sioux he'd encountered weeks before in the Green Mountains.

"I, too, bring the young," the Indian said at last. "We seek the medicine that flows from the old ones."

"It's good," Willie said, nodding at the older men. "The old ways shouldn't be forgotten. So much is fading like a setting sun. It's for the young to remember and pass on what's important."

The three older Sioux dismounted and stepped closer. The old man on the left drew an old red pipe from a bundle and offered it to the younger man.

"We would smoke with you," the Sioux explained, "but we have no tobacco. Our people have been a long time on the plain, and we have not traded in all that time."

"Don!" Willie called. "You still got some tobacco left for that awful pipe of yours?"

"Sure do," Barker said, reaching into his hip pocket and

drawing out a pouch. Pat Nolan took the tobacco and raced to Willie's side. The Indian tossed a bit of it to the four directions, then said a prayer before filling the bowl. Soon Willie sat at one side of a circle. The Sioux boys remained mounted. Their eyes betrayed distrust.

Willie couldn't blame them. Barker waited beside the butchered buffalo with Pat and Tim. Only Chip joined the circle. As each in turn took a draw at the pipe, a strange quiet settled over the circle. Finally the pipe returned to the old man who had filled the pipe.

"I am called Three Eagles," the younger man at his side explained.

"Wil Devlin," Willie said. "You speak English well."

"I lived for a time at the soldier forts," Three Eagles explained. "You also know much. You have lived with the Sioux, the Cheyenne, perhaps the Arapaho?"

"Comanche," Willie explained. "Long ago."

"You carry their marks," Three Eagles observed as Willie again touched the ancient scar on his wrist. "What did they call you?"

"Bright Star," Willie whispered, recalling the shine that had once filled his eyes. "That was long ago. The brightness has faded."

"And these Comanches who named you?"

"The earth knows them no longer," Willie said grimly. "There will be no sons to remember them."

"Yes, death walks the plain now," Three Eagles observed. "It is good you teach your sons."

"These are not my blood," Willie said, touching Chip lightly on the shoulder.

Three Eagles spoke to the older men. The pipe bearer gazed at the sky, then closed his eyes a few minutes. Then the old man slowly spoke a string of melodic Sioux phrases. Chip grinned, and Three Eagles turned to Willie.

"He says a man doesn't choose his father," Three Eagles interpreted, smiling faintly at Chip. "We know this boy. He stands at your side now, as a son should. You teach the others as a father would. Among the Brule, they would call you *até*, father. Often Wakan Tanka, the grandfather spirit, makes a man's path long and hard. He brings burdens a man does not seek. It isn't wise to turn away from the struggle."

"No, but it wears on a man."

Three Eagles nodded.

The old man spoke again, and Three Eagles grinned.

"He says a man with three sons needs a wife," Three Eagles explained. "Buffalo Hump has a granddaughter, young and pretty, and he says a man of many horses and three sons could do well to trade for her."

Willie grinned, and Chip laughed. Before Willie could think of a reply, Chip spoke. This time the old man laughed as well, then took the pipe and started it around the circle again. When it returned to Buffalo Hump, the old man extinguished it and returned the unsmoked tobacco.

"It is well," Three Eagles spoke as he clasped Willie's arm. "Go in peace, Bright Star."

"You also," Willie whispered.

The Sioux departed, and Willie turned to Chip.

"What did you tell the old man?" Willie asked.

"That you've got a white woman back at your lodge," Chip explained.

"He wasn't laughing about that," Willie declared.

"Well, I told him if the girl was pretty enough, I had a few horses I might spare myself."

Willie grinned and ushered the boy back toward their companions. The Sioux set off westward, following the buffalo. And for a time peace settled over the plain.

But for how long? Willie wondered.

While they packed the last of the meat on the travois, a cloud of dust attested to riders approaching from the east. Not Sioux this time, Willie's instincts told him, and they, as usual, were correct. At the head of a column of soldiers pranced a stiff-necked cavalry major.

Chip jumped atop his horse and rode out to have a look. He returned with the major and a grizzled old sergeant.

"When I saw that barebacked boy, I thought you might be Sioux," the major said, scowling as he gazed at Chip's long, unkempt hair. "What're you doing out this way anyway?"

"We chase down range ponies," Don Barker said, stepping over. "I own the SC Ranch back a way."

"Don't look to be runnin' ponies down just now," the sergeant grumbled. "Buffs?"

"That's right," Willie answered. "We needed fresh meat."

"Sure," the major said. "Didn't kill many, though. Shame. We been chasing a band of Sioux. Just a few renegades left out this way, you know. Soon we'll have the buffalo killed off, and even the real stubborn ones will have to come in by first snow. It's time we got this country properly settled. Bring in some farmers, plant corn, and we'll have ourselves another Kansas."

Willie started to reply, but Barker spoke first.

"You boys have a fair ride, Major," Barker called. "Watch out those Sioux don't find you first."

"Little chance of that," the major declared. "I've got scouts out."

Sure, you do, Willie thought as the soldiers continued their march. With fresh tracks all over the place, the fools didn't even ask us if we'd seen Indians.

He thought no more of the soldiers, though. Three Eagles wasn't after trouble, not with old men and boys along. And there was work to be done.

By the time the last of the meat was packed on the travois and Willie had the company mounted and heading homeward, the sun was hanging low in the western sky. The boys argued for making an early camp down by the river.

"I stink of blood, Wil," Pat complained.

"He's right," Chip admitted. "Tildy won't ever let us in her kitchen without a scrubbin', and it's growin' dark. Let's make camp and fry up some o' those steaks."

Barker quickly agreed, and Chip led the way to a grove of cottonwoods down on the riverbank.

It troubled Willie to stop. He'd promised to be back by nightfall. The boys were clearly exhausted, though, and Willie was tired, too. He climbed off his horse, shed his clothes, and joined the others in the river. They lay in the refreshing water a full hour. Then Chip rose and hurried to start dinner.

The boy mixed a bit of spice with the meat, then dug up some wild onions and turnips to round out the meal. Willie found himself more amazed daily at young Chip's resourcefulness. Pat, in fine fashion as usual, devoured his steak and crawled to Chip on bended knee.

"Chippewa Colter, will ya marry me?" Pat asked, pleading with pretended passion. "You can cook and tend a man's aches. Will you share my winter lodge?"

"Me?" Chip responded in a humorous falsetto. "Me? I'm part Indian, remember? I won't wed a puny white eye like you, Pat Nolan! Watch yourself, too. My father taught me to deal harshly with any boy who trifles with my virtue."

"What?" Pat asked, laughing.

Chip drew out a long knife, made a short slash at the air, and the whole outfit fell to the ground laughing.

That night the camp rocked with laughter and high tales. Willie contributed neither. He again spread his blankets away from the others, and his eyes watched a neat row of campfires punctuating the distant darkness. Later, when the boys took to their beds, the wind turned, and voices echoed along the Sweetwater.

"Soldiers," Willie grumbled. More trouble.

An eering feeling crept up his spine, and he suddenly gazed eastward, toward the ranch. He could detect pinpricks of light in that direction, too, a pair of camps a few miles apart. Perhaps it was the SC and Statham's cattle operation.

No, he told himself. The intervening hills would mask Statham's place.

Willie thought to rouse Barker, then ride on alone and see for himself. But it had been a long day, and he was as tired as the others. He yawned, then kicked off his boots and pulled his blanket tight against his chest. Whatever it was would wait for tomorrow.

CHAPTER 19

Being just a few miles short of the SC, Willie convinced his companions to forego breakfast and head along home. They rode at a brisk pace, and, the morning dew still clung to the high grass when they topped the hills that formed the ranch's western boundary. Shortly thereafter Willie heard a horse whine from the river. To his surprise, the white mare galloped by, tauntingly dipping her head.

"I'll fetch her," Tim promised, darting toward the animal. Pat charged after his friend.

"Well?" Barker asked.

"I'm headed home," Willie declared. Chip and Barker followed. Soon, though, Chip spotted two stray mustangs, and it took the three of them to round up the renegades. By that time Pat and Tim had the white in hand, and Willie led his reassembled outfit on to the house, grumbling bitterly that the Redmonds ought to be able to watch a corral at least.

They were still a hundred yards from the house when the hair on Willie's neck began to rise. It wasn't the sight of the empty corrals that troubled him. Willie expected as much. But it was out of character for the place to be so quiet, and even more so for Tildy not to have a kettle on the stove. Nary a wisp of smoke rose from the stovepipe. In fact, there wasn't a sign of life to the entire place.

"Wait here," Willie cautioned as he rode on alone. The boys drove the horses into the corrals, but Barker remained mounted. His eyes followed Willie's every movement, and the former freight guard had drawn a Winchester from his saddle scabbard.

Willie called to Tildy, then shouted louder.

"Tildy? Gump? You there?"

He then dismounted, drew his pistol, and stepped inside.

It was clear there'd been trouble. Gear was strewn everywhere. Cups and plates were thrown on the floor, and linings had been torn from coats. A table stood on one end, and bullet holes ventilated one wall.

Willie emerged to find Don Barker nervously gazing at the dugout. Chip stood in the doorway, shaking his head.

"There's no sign of anybody," Barker declared. "But there's sure been a fight. Any fool can read the holes in that wall, Wil. Where could they have gotten to?"

Willie hoped for the best, but inside the doubts were gnawing at him. He wanted to believe old Gump had somehow gotten the others away. Pat found a bloodstained saddle blanket at the corral, though.

"Where are they?" Pat asked, flinging the blanket against the wall of the house. "Lord, Wil, we should've come on like you said."

"Maybe," Barker admitted. "But that blood's maybe a day old, Pat. Could've happened the afternoon we left."

"Either way, there ought to be some sign of 'em," Pat complained. "What's happened here?"

The answers came soon enough. A solitary rider rode up from the south. He halted fifty feet out and waved his friendly intentions.

"I'm George Statham," the young man explained. "My pa's got the ranch down south. He bought some horses off you, remember?"

"I do," Willie answered, starting toward the rider. George Statham had one arm wrapped in white cloth, and a purple bruise occupied the left side of his forehead. He was maybe seventeen, but the excitement in his voice caused him to appear younger.

"I come for a fellow name of Wil Devlin," George explained. "You him?"

"I am," Willie answered.

"Pa said I should fetch you soon as you rode in."

"First tell me what's happened," Willie insisted. "Where are my—"

"Was outlaws, Mr. Devlin," George said, gazing uneasily at the hills to the west. "They hit us, too."

"When?" Pat called.

"Close to midmornin' yesterday," George explained. "They came from nowhere. Ten or more of 'em, I'd guess. We had some soldiers through just before, and we thought it was them, come back to chat. Wasn't. They tore through here like a bunch o' angry hornets. Killed my brother Zeke, Uncle Lacy..."

"They have names, these fellows?" Willie asked as Chip led the horses out of the corral.

"I guess they do, but I don't know 'em, 'cept for the two got kilt and the one leadin' 'em."

"And him?"

"Oh, we'll be a long time rememberin' that one," George said bitterly. "Gunned down Zeke like you'd shoot a mad dog. Not hard to pick him out of a crowd. No, sir!"

"Why?"

"Just had one arm, you see. Others called him Ashton."

"Not Ashton," Willie said, shaking with rage. "Ashley. Shadrack Ashley, curse his soul."

"You know him?"

"I've crossed his trail... and will again," Willie muttered as he climbed atop his saddle. "Let's go, George."

In seconds the SC crew was galloping after George Statham toward the neighboring ranch. Along the way Willie thought of Ashley's taunting words, of the way he coldly shot down Vance Bonner at Rock Creek.

He won't get away this time, Willie vowed. And if he's harmed Tildy...

The Statham ranch reminded Willie of a Virginia battlefield. The barn was just a heap of ashes. Every window was shot out of the house, and dead livestock was scattered here and there.

Gordon Statham met them on his porch. The rancher rested his weight on two forked cottonwood limbs that served as crutches.

"They hit you bad," Willie observed.

"Middlin'," Statham said, bitterly staring at the ashes of his barn. "I lost my home to Sherman back in sixty-four. I was burned out in Julesburg by Cheyenne. Lost my eldest girl in that one. Now my second boy, just fourteen, shot for no good reason under the sun. Yeah, middlin' hard by Georgia scales."

"How'd they do it?" Willie asked, afraid to ask the question rising on his lips.

"A dozen of 'em maybe," Statham explained. "Came on us like lightnin'. My brother Lacy and Zeke were down before we even knew what was happenin'. They trapped me and George in the shed, but we had a pair of shotguns. Sent two of 'em to an early reward, we did. The rest got discouraged, and it settled down some for a time. When they found they couldn't get to the house, they fired the barn and rode off. Once the smoke cleared, I sent my boys to have a look at your place."

"And?" Willie asked, trembling.

"George?" Statham said, turning to his son.

"Was me and Henry found the first ones," George said, avoiding Willie's intense gaze. "Your wranglers, down at the corral. I guess they were tryin' to get to their horses, or maybe they just meant to let the stock loose. Anyway, looked to me like one went down, and the other one tried to help him."

"They were brothers," Barker pointed out.

"Ashton, or Ashley, or whatever his name was had 'em cut on some 'fore they died. Guess he was lookin' for money or some such."

"And the girl?" Willie asked. "The old man?"

"They put up a fight," George said, swallowing hard. "Only the old one was still breathin' when Henry and I rode up. He was shot up fierce, Mr. Devlin, five, six times. I don't see how he hung on. Kept tellin' us to see to the girl. I guess he was hangin' on, hopin' they wouldn't get to her."

"But they did, didn't they?" Willie asked.

"Well, I don't know what happened inside that house," George confessed. "Be my guess somebody shot through the wall and kilt her. She just had the one bullet in her, Mr. Devlin, and there was a dead man in the doorway with his chest full o' buckshot. They didn't get close enough to bother her any."

"Just close enough to kill her," Willie said, coughing as his throat constricted.

"Why don't you come down from there and have some tea?" a kind-faced woman who appeared in the doorway asked. "Gordon, you've no brain at all, keepin' these folks sittin' on their horses all this time!"

Statham motioned toward the door, and Willie dismounted. But while the others filed inside the house, Willie remained on the porch.

"Where is she?" Willie asked Statham.

"Emma?" Statham said, turning to the woman.

"I'll show you," she told Willie. After issuing instructions to a slender girl of thirteen or so, Emma Statham conducted Willie around the side of the house and along toward a grove of recently planted apple seedlings. Beyond them were six fresh graves, all marked with crossed white pickets.

"I didn't know what names to have George etch," she explained. "I took care to note who was laid where. The older gentleman is next to my Zeke, and beside him lies his daughter."

"She wasn't his daughter," Willie explained. "Not by blood anyway. But in a way—well, I guess she was."

"The two others are on the right there. The bald fellow is on the end."

"I'll write the names down for you."

"Here," she said, passing Willie a kerchief to dab the tears forming in his eyes. He shook his head, though, and blinked away the tears. "I've got paper and a pencil, if you care to write them now," Mrs. Statham added. "Sometimes it helps to have somethin' to do."

"Yes," Willie agreed. He began with Curly Redmond. Willie couldn't recall the bald wrangler's real name, and perhaps it didn't matter anyway. Ned was probably short for something, too. Oh, well, a short name for a short life. Willie printed Mathilde Bonner neatly in spite of a quivering hand. Then he wrote Nathaniel Barlow, called Gump.

"I'm sure George will happily carve the names," Mrs. Statham assured Willie. "He does a fine job, don't you think?"

Willie noted the woman's sadness and nodded his head. She then left him alone, and he knelt beside the crosses.

He rubbed his eyes and touched the splintery side of Gump's cross.

"You did all you could, old-timer," Willie whispered. "I wasn't there. But I'm here to do what's left, and I promise you I will."

Then he gazed at the like cross marking Tildy's resting place.

"I didn't even get a chance to say good-bye," Willie whispered. "But then I never was much good at it anyhow. I guess it wasn't to be, Tildy. Me and dreams—well, we just never could take the same trail. We thought we were headed for better times when we left Rock Creek, but I don't guess you can ever leave trouble very far behind."

Willie rose sadly and swallowed his sadness. In its place his chest swelled with a fiery rage.

"Ashley!" he shouted, fingering the handle of the Colt on his hip. "You're dead this minute, and you don't even know it."

Willie returned to the house long enough to talk Gordon Statham out of a box of Winchester shells.

"You can't mean to do it on your own, not with those

boys," Statham argued. "Those soldiers aren't far away, and—"

"I left it to the bluecoats once before," Willie explained. "I'll settle accounts with him myself this time."

"There are six or seven of 'em left, Devlin."

"You got shells to spare or not?" Willie asked.

Statham located two boxes. Willie took them both.

As he packed the shells in his saddlebags and prepared to head out, Don Barker held him back.

"We'll all of us go," Barker declared. "They were my friends, too."

"All of us?" Willie asked. "What all of us? Pat? Young Tim? Chip? No, you stay and build that ranch. Keep her dream alive for me, Don. Something ought to survive, don't you think?"

Barker nodded sadly, then stepped back. Tim Phipps walked over and rested a hand on Willie's shoulder.

"Yeah, I know," Willie said. "I kind of liked the notion of being a father myself, Tim. But you've been growing yourself a while now, and old Don there's a good man to follow."

"Sure," Tim said, clasping Willie's hand.

Chip Colter could not be put off with a handshake, though.

"You said to learn the old ways," Chip reminded Willie. "Well, I know the Sioux way. Your trouble is my trouble. I can track as well as anybody alive."

"And you can die, too," Willie said, gripping the slender-shouldered youngster with both hands. "You don't understand, Chip. Stay and grow old. I won't lead any more boys to their deaths. I have enough faces haunting my dreams. Do you understand?"

"I understand," Chip said, shaking loose. "I have lost another father."

"No, Chip," Willie argued. "I'd never have made one. My road's too rocky for me to carry anyone along."

Pat Nolan then struck up a mournful tune on his mouth organ, and Willie climbed atop his horse.

"Wil?" Pat called as his companions followed Barker into the house.

"I got to do it, Pat," Willie said, nodding sadly to the boy.

"I'd come along if you'd have me."

"Pat," Willie said, forcing a grin to his face, "you're game as anybody I ever met, but you couldn't hit a bull buff from fifty feet. There's only death waiting out there for you."

"I'm not afraid."

"Neither was Vance, and now he's dead. You'll make a good man if you give yourself half a chance."

"You'll be back, won't you?"

"I wouldn't bank on that," Willie mumbled. "You stick with Don Barker. He's a good man to learn from."

"So're you," Pat declared.

Me? Willie thought as he turned his horse westward. Me? The only thing I have to teach is pain and death. I know them well. They're my only companions now.

CHAPTER 20

Willie picked up Ashley's trail right away. The arrogant outlaw made no effort to conceal his tracks. He rode across open ground into the hills, and Willie reached the camp where Ashley had passed the night by midafternoon.

Willie examined the place carefully. He counted eight mounds of pine needles that had certainly bedded outlaws.

"Only eight?" he muttered. Well, the odds were long, but then Ashley wasn't expecting pursuit, was he?

By dusk the trail led Willie into a series of ravines and low hills to the south. He moved more cautiously. Ashley had slowed the pace, for the indentations made by hooves showed a plodding, deliberate gait now. Willie drew out his Winchester and rested it on one knee. In the twilight, he could see only shadows. The wind carried the scent of wood smoke, though, and he thought he heard voices just ahead.

A lot of years had passed since Willie learned to stalk prey in the spotted hills of his native Texas. In that time he'd learned to sniff out ambush. He blended into shadows and crept through the scrub pines until he could finally detect a small fire up ahead. His eyes then identified a foreign shape to his right. He cautiously stepped that way, then bent down to examine it.

The body of a bearded man in his mid-thirties stared

lifelessly toward the sky. His bare chest and abdomen were sliced open, and his scalp lock had been cut away.

Willie stared coldly at the corpse. The dead man wore Gump's boots.

So, Ashley, you've run into trouble of another kind, Willie thought. And there are but seven of you left.

Just ahead two younger men lay scalped as well. Willie recognized one from the Rock Creek raid.

Five now, he thought. And when I finish, none.

In spite of the fading darkness, or perhaps on account of it, Willie was able to slip unnoticed upon an encampment of sorts a hundred yards down the trail. A riderless horse stood a strange vigil at the edge of the clearing. Willie readied himself to confront Shad Ashley. But it was not Ashley who sat beside the camp's solitary fire.

"Three Eagles?" Willie called out in surprise as he turned the barrel of the rifle away from the Indian. Buffalo Hump, the ancient pipe bearer, sat propped against a nearby tree. Two dark-browed teenagers tended the old man.

"You're not welcome here, white man," Three Eagles asserted. "This is a place of mourning."

"I'm sorry to intrude," Willie said respectfully. "I ride in search of some men. Three of 'em are dead back a ways."

"The others will soon be dead also," Three Eagles said as he tossed a stick on the fire. "I will cut their dark hearts out!"

"There are five left by my count," Willie said, settling in across the fire from the Sioux. "Too many for a single man."

"And yet you hunt alone."

"Yes," Willie admitted. "Pain sends a man off without thinking sometimes. It gives him strength, too."

"Your sons?" Three Eagles asked anxiously. "They, too, are not . . ."

"No," Willie said, swallowing. "The woman who would have given me sons. An old man who rode with me.

Two others who never did anyone harm. A boy who was like a brother was killed in the spring by these same ones."

"I read it in your eyes," Three Eagles said. "Come, see my heart broken."

The Sioux led Willie to six stiffening bodies. One was a weathered old man who'd been struck in the chest with a single bullet. The others were of a tender age. Young, once wide-eyed and eager, they now slept in a terrible silence. Knives and bullets had plucked the life from each.

"My sister's son, who knew me as father," Three Eagles explained, touching the cold arm of a slender boy who, save for the round hole in his side, might have been dozing peacefully. "My own child, taken this day from his father's side," Three Eagles added, kneeling beside a second boy.

"Your loss is great," Willie said, shuddering. "Mine, too. If there's justice in this life, the guilty will suffer greatly for their actions."

"Justice?" Three Eagles called with reddening eyes. "Buffalo Hump, who speaks to the spirits, lies dying. We, he and I, brought these boys here to learn the old ways. Instead they have learned the new."

Yes, Willie thought. Death and pain.

"They came by night," Three Eagles mumbled as he rose to his feet. "Like coyotes, they crept upon us. Their leader—"

"Was a one-armed snake name of Ashley. I near killed him twice. I won't fail to finish the task this time."

"Your heart is hard, my friend, as mine is, but his eyes were dark and full of killing. He won't be easy to find, and it will be harder killing him."

"Not for me," Willie said bitterly. "A man without a heart never finds killing too difficult. Besides, it's a trade I've practiced before."

Three Eagles appeared less than convinced, but he didn't argue. Instead the two men returned to the campfire. One of the boys brought over some dried venison, and Willie ate a bit of it. He'd tasted nothing save hard news all day, and his stomach welcomed the food.

After eating, Three Eagles sat beside Buffalo Hump and listened as the old man muttered a string of phrases.

"He sees them," Three Eagles explained to Willie. "Five white men. They ride to the river and beyond."

"Where?" Willie asked.

"To the place of their death," Three Eagles added. "An evil place where the dark spirits dwell."

"Where's that?" Willie asked, gazing intently at Buffalo Hump.

"I, too, see it," one of the boys added, growing pale. "There is a great hole in the earth that has swallowed the evil one. All about are high places, sacred to Wakan Tanka."

"Devil's Gate," Willie said, feeling an icy sensation creep over him.

"Yes, the haunted place," Three Eagles agreed. "They will be a long time getting there by the path they choose. We will wait for them."

Another might have argued against leaving a clear trail in order to follow the vision of a dying old man. Not Willie. He'd seen the power in dreams, and he knew it would be like Shad Ashley to choose a place like Devil's Gate after tangling with Indians.

Buffalo Hump then began chanting. Willie knew none of the words, but it was clearly a death chant. The old man's eyes glazed over, and he slumped to one side.

"I'll cut limbs for scaffolds," Willie said, rising. "We'll place them high in the old way."

"High, yes," Three Eagles agreed. "But there is no need of poles. A cliff nearby will hold them dearly. White men tear down the scaffolds for firewood, and they rob the dead of their weapons and clothing. Some do worse."

Willie frowned. It was true enough. Hadn't his own brother desecrated the old Comanche burial place high above the Brazos?

Three Eagles and the boys then wrapped Buffalo Hump in a blanket and carried the old man off. Willie didn't follow. He knew it was a solemn, secret time for the Sioux.

Instead Willie slipped his shirt from his shoulders and drew out a knife. He recalled how Yellow Shirt had once drawn blood to show his resolve. Willie now made a shallow cut in his chest, then another. Blood trickled down to his belly, touching the dim red scar left by a Yank saber so very long ago.

"If I'm to go to my death here, then I am ready," he whispered to the stars overhead. "I've walked with death often these past few years. I don't fear it. Truth is, it might offer some peace. But live or die, I have to silence this storm of pain that calls itself Shad Ashley. Please, Lord, let us catch him and put an end to all this suffering."

When Three Eagles returned at last with his two young companions, Willie lay beside the fire chanting a half-remembered Comanche song. Three Eagles roused him.

"You were right about the name," the Sioux said somberly. "You are Bright Star no longer. Now I will call you Two Scars, for the marks on the outside and the deeper ones within."

"It's a good name," Willie quickly agreed.

The three Sioux also chanted. Willie knew their prayers were much the same as his own. When all of them took to their blankets, Willie closed his eyes and listened to the crickets. Bitterness ate at his insides. There was no music to the night. No stars shone above. No, he was left there alone, surrounded by the chilling dark and possessed by the terrible purpose at hand.

CHAPTER 21

It was a hard two-day ride to Devil's Gate on fresh horses. It took Willie and the Indians longer. For one thing, they were wary of running across Ashley's raiders in the open. Worse, the first day out a squad of cavalry patrolled the best crossing of the Sweetwater, and Three Eagles swung well to the west to avoid the soldiers.

As they continued onward, Willie couldn't help feeling their chances of catching Ashley slipping away. Here I am, Willie thought, riding along, guided by an old man's vision, trailing as desperate a band of outlaws as any I've known, with only an Indian and a couple of half-grown boys to help mete out justice. It was clearly crazy.

The journey wasn't made easier by a scarcity of food. They didn't dare build a campfire, and cold nights blended with long days to send a world of misery through the four of them.

The third morning after leaving Three Eagles's camp, Willie spotted Ashley's trail. Five horses had recently ridden along the north bank of the river. A bit farther on, Willie detected two other riders merging with the others. They led a column of heavily laden animals, likely packhorses.

"So, now there are seven," Three Eagles grumbled

when Willie pointed out the tracks. "Soon they will be in the rocks."

"It's time to ride hard," Willie declared. "You up to it?"

"Watch me, Two Scars. I rode this land when you still wet yourself."

Willie managed half a grin as he urged his horse after the Sioux ponies. The four of them set off at a light gallop that swung north and west, around Ashley's flank, and on to Devil's Gate.

As they threaded their way through the boulder-strewn countryside, Willie recalled Gump's old tale of the Shoshoni monster. He felt the same torment that devil must have known. A hundred small lances seemed to prick every inch of him. And whenever he closed his eyes, he envisioned Ashley's taunting eyes, saw the lifeless faces of Vance, Tildy, and Gump.

I've lost them all, Willie thought. It's as if a thief has crept in and stolen all the good I've been able to find. Fresh fury filled his chest, and he rode on with new resolve.

The great gap in the rocks known as Devil's Gate greeted them late that afternoon. The place transmitted an eerie feeling, and Willie read the uneasy faces of his companions. They would never have chosen such a spot for an ambush. Ashley knew the dread the Plains tribes held for the place. It's what made it a perfect choice to wait for the outlaws.

"We have beaten them here," Three Eagles announced as he led the way through the rocks and along toward the base of the high wall broken by the gap. "Now we must ready ourselves."

Willie spread his blankets off to one side. While the Indians smoked the pipe and chanted, Willie cleaned and oiled his pistol and the long-barreled Winchester. He watched with interest as the boys tied up the tails of their horses and exchanged their buckskins for bright red breechclouts. Three Eagles tied three feathers in his hair, then painted his face black as death.

Yes, they're taking this seriously, Willie thought. The boys chanted reverently. Willie prayed his own silent entreaties. Then Three Eagles spoke to the youngsters in a calm, severe voice.

"What did you tell 'em?" Willie asked afterward.

"To watch out for the one-armed one," Three Eagles explained. "His eyes carry death."

"Are they any different from mine?" Willie asked.

"They are different," the Sioux said, smiling grimly at his young companions. "Your eyes speak of death as an end to your pain, Two Scars. The one-armed coyote feeds on death as a man with a great hunger."

Willie also had a hunger just then. He longed to see Ashley's men ride down into the rocks, come into this spider's web that was waiting for them.

Three Eagles sent the boys out to watch for the expected outlaws. Willie would rather the boys'd stayed to the shadows, but Three Eagles said young eyes were needed just then. Willie didn't argue. The guns were ready now, reloaded and eager to deal death to Ashley's murdering raiders.

It was nearly dusk when Walks the Mountains, the elder of the boys, brought word of Ashley.

"They ride in a line," Three Eagles told Willie. "Soon they will be here. Come."

Willie needed no second urging. He took his rifle, stuffed his pockets with extra shells, and set off for the rocks.

The ambush would have been easier in daylight. With sunlight fading, it was a challenge to get into position and fire accurately. Ashley himself, together with two men, brought up the rear. The lead riders escorted a pack train laden with purloined goods.

Three Eagles said nothing. There was no need. His eyes told everything. They flashed to the right, and Walks the Mountains led the other boy along to watch the end of the column. The Sioux nodded to his left, and Willie took position behind a boulder and waited. Then, as the outlaws closed the distance, laughing and recounting their exploits, Three Eagles gave a shout and shot the third rider in line off his horse.

The Sioux boys whooped and dove into the midst of Ashley's column, slashing out with knives and screaming like avenging devils.

Willie remained in the rocks as the line of riders dissolved in confusion. He waited calmly until one slapped his horse past. Willie fired, and the fleeing outlaw's head snapped back.

In a matter of minutes, four of the raiders were dead. The survivors, including Shad Ashley, jumped clear of their horses and scrambled into a rocky ravine. Horses fell, screaming, or raced past, raising clouds of dust and rock. Confusion spread through the darkness. A half-naked figure charged the ravine, then spun awkwardly as a volley of rifle fire met him.

"Ayyyyahh!" Three Eagles cried furiously.

The Sioux rushed out and dragged his fallen companion to cover. Willie, meanwhile, crawled to the far end of the ravine and started toward the remaining outlaws.

For a moment an eerie silence settled over Devil's Gate. It provided a chance for one of the raiders to race along the edge of the ravine and try to slip away unnoticed. Willie raised his pistol and blasted the fleeing renegade. The raider clutched his throat and tumbled into the pit of the ravine.

"Lord, Jack? Jack?" a voice called from the opposite end of the ravine.

Willie's hands trembled as he examined the fallen raider. It was too dark to see the speaker's face, but that voice was all too familiar.

"He's dead, Ashley!" Willie shouted. "You'll be joining him soon enough."

"Who's that?" Ashley called as his companion made a break for a nearby horse. The raider howled in pain, then screamed horribly as Three Eagles took a knife to him.

"You're all that's left, eh?" Willie asked. "Like back at

Rock Creek, only there're no boys left for you to shoot, nobody to cover you. Remember yet, huh, Ashley? Remember when they took that arm? Well?"

"Devlin!" Ashley shouted.

The voice contained no anger now. Fear set the shadowy shape scurrying deeper into the gully. Ashley was doing his best to dig his way into the ground. Willie crept cautiously onward, warily eyeing Ashley. The killer remained still, but he was far from taken. A rifle barrel protruded from the rocks.

I've come too far to die short of seeing you dead, Willie silently told Shad Ashley. Willie blinked away a wave of recollections and continued. Three Eagles was closing in from the opposite side. Ashley must have sensed that, for he suddenly sprung to his feet and bolted from the ravine.

Willie's hand moved quick as lightning. His eye fixed Ashley in a deadly gaze, and the pistol barrel swung rapidly. Willie's finger pressed the trigger, and the Colt exploded. The bullet tore through the gray haze and shattered Shad Ashley's right kneecap.

"Ahhh!" Ashley screamed as he stumbled, writhing, to the ground. The outlaw remained there a moment, then tried to drag himself along. Willie fired again. A bullet sliced off Ashley's toe.

"Going someplace, Ashley?" Willie called from the shadows. "Remember what you said you'd do to me that day at Willow Creek? Like to see for yourself how it'd feel?"

"Devlin, don't!" Ashley pleaded as Willie fired again, this time sending a bullet into the sand a few inches from Ashley's right ear.

"Leave him to me," Three Eagles called, creeping toward the prone outlaw. "I will show him the way a coyote should die."

"Lord, Devlin, you travelin' with Indians?" Ashley cried. "You can't mean to let 'em cut on me. You're a white man, for God's sake."

"Don't speak to me of mercy!" Willie barked. "Half a

week back you shot down a boy of fourteen in front of his own mama! You never showed anybody mercy as I can remember. I don't figure I owe you any now."

"Please," Ashley muttered, pulling himself to his knees and firing wildly. "End it quick!"

"Not quick," Three Eagles insisted.

Ashley turned his pistol toward the Indian, but Willie shot the gun from the killer's hand. The dust began to settle, and Ashley stood out in the pale light like some phantom horror. He fought to grip his pistol with bleeding fingers, but he only managed to pitch forward.

"I made a mistake not findin' you first!" Ashley screamed.

"You did!" Willie hollered back.

"Devlin, you devil, finish it!" Ashley yelled.

"I'll leave that to my friends, the Sioux."

Three Eagles howled. The boy whooped. Ashley slumped over, then drew out a small pistol and waved it blindly. Willie ducked, then looked on with wide eyes as Ashley pressed the barrel to his own forehead and fired. The outlaw grunted, then fell backward, dead.

The Sioux were on him in a flash, but Three Eagles pulled his companions back.

"We can't take his scalp," Three Eagles explained. "The spirits touched him at the end. There are scalps elsewhere, though."

"And the other boy, Walks the Mountains?" Willie asked.

Three Eagles frowned, and Willie knew another body would rest in the high places. He stepped over and stared down at the lifeless figure that had so tormented him across the Sweetwater country, who had robbed him of what gentleness he'd managed to find.

"It's over, Ashley," Willie muttered, turning the corpse face down so that its glaring eyes could no longer haunt him. "So many are dead, and for what? For what, Ashley?"

EPILOGUE

If it was true that Devil's Gate was a haunted place, then it seemed a fit place for a Satan like Ashley to die. That night Three Eagles and his young companion, Lone Hawk, cut lengths of cottonwood, and Willie helped erect a scaffold. They rolled Walks the Mountains in a blanket and set his frail form atop the burial platform.

Three Eagles placed assorted weapons at the boy's side, then hung a lance adorned with six scalps across the far end of the scaffold.

"Here sleeps a brave one," Three Eagles declared.

"May he find his peace," Willie whispered.

Lone Hawk began chanting, and Three Eagles led the way back down the hillside to where a small fire burned. Ashley's packs had provided a generous dinner, and now Three Eagles filled the red pipe with what he called sweet grass.

"We will make a good smoke this night," Three Eagles said, performing the pipe ritual slowly, carefully, explaining little of it to Willie. He nonetheless comprehended the solemnity of the moment, and he puffed the pipe with the respect expected of an honored guest.

Three Eagles and Lone Hawk then cut themselves and chanted the mourning songs merited by the loss of their young friend. Willie left them to share the sadness while he set off up the hill. From there he could gaze southward, toward the Texas that again seemed a world away. It wasn't Texas that flooded his thoughts, though. He was thinking first of Ellen, then of the yellow-haired girl who might have breathed life into their old dream.

"Tildy, what cruel wind was it carried you away?" he whispered. "What jokester Fate brought us so close to being happy just to pull you away so suddenly?"

There was, of course, no answer but the whining wind. Willie remained there, staring into the black, empty night until the weariness swept him away into a muted sleep.

He awoke to discover Three Eagles perched on the hill beside him. Willie shook himself to life, then nodded solemnly toward the Indian.

"Where will you go, Two Scars?" the Sioux asked. "Have you a home to go to? The boys would welcome your return?"

"I've got no home," Willie explained. "The boys are better off forgetting me."

"Then where will you go?"

"On," Willie mumbled. As always, he thought. On and on until death frees me from the torment of life.

"How far must you ride?" Three Eagles asked.

"How far does any man ride?" Willie asked in turn. "Until I find my way. Or death eases the pain."

"Yes, it is so," the Indian agreed. "I, too, feel death's shadow upon the plain. Come, seek the high country with Lone Hawk and me. My people camp on the Bighorn. There is good hunting there, and in winter, the world is born over."

"Winter's hard up high," Willie muttered. "I've been there."

"Yes, but it is a place to feel close to the sky spirits."

"Perhaps," Willie admitted. "Perhaps."

He stared again southward. Autumn was on the wind now. Summer neared its sunburned conclusion.

"It's a good place, the Bighorn," Willie recalled. Once it had brought peace. For a time. Now?

"Look there!" Three Eagles exclaimed, pointing overhead as a great golden eagle turned slow circles in the morning sky.

Willie recalled old Yellow Shirt pointing out just such an eagle as the best of omens.

"It marks a journey well begun," the old Comanche had explained.

"You will come?" Three Eagles asked.

"I've got no other direction," Willie answered. "One place is as good as another, I suppose."

"Perhaps," Three Eagles said, grinning. "But the eagle marks the way."

Yes, Willie thought.

And so he rode out that morning with Three Eagles and young Lone Hawk, leading the packhorses along as they wove their way westward, north of the Sweetwater, toward the Bighorn Mountains that towered far in the distance.

Willie glanced back but once. There was no point to searching the past for what was gone forever. Tildy was dead, and Ellen was lost. Willie—well, he was somewhere between the two, carried along on the wind, following a wandering eagle into the distant unknown.

ABOUT THE AUTHOR

G. Clifton Wisler comes by his interest in the West naturally. Born in Oklahoma and raised in Texas, he discovered early on a fascination for the history of the region. His first novel, MY BROTHER, THE WIND, received a nomination for the American Book Award in 1980. Among the many others that have followed are THUNDER ON THE TENNESSEE, winner of the Western Writers of America Spur Award for Best Western Juvenile Book of 1983; WINTER OF THE WOLF, a Spur finalist in 1982; and Delamer Westerns THE TRIDENT BRAND, STARR'S SHOWDOWN, PURGATORY, ABREGO CANYON, THE WAYWARD TRAIL, and SWEETWATER FLATS. In addition to his writing, Wisler frequently speaks to school groups and conducts writing clinics. He lives in Garland, Texas where he is active in Boy Scouts.